Ashton's Dancing Dreams

Also by Camryn, Kaitlyn, and Olivia Pitts

Ansley's Big Bake Off (Book 1—The Daniels Sisters Series)

And check out these titles by Alena Pitts!

The Lena in the Spotlight Series

Book 1—*Hello Stars*

Book 2—*Day Dreams and Movie Screens*

Book 3—*Shining Night*

faithgirlz

Ashton's Dancing Dreams

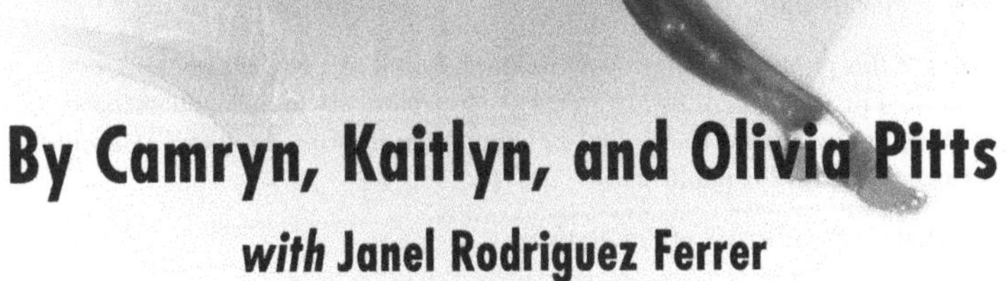

By Camryn, Kaitlyn, and Olivia Pitts

with Janel Rodriguez Ferrer

ZONDERKIDZ

Ashton's Dancing Dreams

Requests for information should be addressed to:
Zonderkidz, *3900 Sparks Dr. SE, Grand Rapids, Michigan 49546*

Library of Congress Cataloging-in-Publication Data
Softcover ISBN 978-0-310-76961-3
Library of Congress Control Number: 2020939008

Art direction: Diane Mielke
Interior design: Denise Froehlich

Printed in the United States of America

20 21 22 23 24 LSC 10 9 8 7 6 5 4 3 2 1

From Camryn:

To my mommy—for being my joy.

To Lovie and Kaity—for being my amazing partners!

And to Alena—for being my biggest sister and my inspiration.

From For Girls Like You:

To Roberta, for keeping the mission fresh and moving.

To Nicole, for keeping the vision at the forefront and the picture clear.

To Janel, for continuing to express the kingdom in all of its beauty through your beautiful writing and storytelling.

Chapter 1

My dad, sisters, and I were all in the car, just about to pull up to school, when my favorite song came on the radio—"God is Good," by our favorite singer, Mallory Winston.

"Oooh! Turn it up! Turn it up, Daddy!" My three sisters all spoke at once.

Ansley started swaying to the music. Lena (the eldest) and Amber (my twin) started singing along. I closed my eyes to listen to the lyrics:

When they gave me the bad news
I didn't know what to do.
And I wondered what to say.
Do I laugh or do I cry?
Do I scream or do I sigh?
Or do I just kneel down and pray?

As I kept my eyes closed, I imagined a dance to go along with the words to the song. Daydreaming like this had become one of my favorite things to do lately. It was fun for me because I was taking classes in lyrical dance (a way of acting out a story with dance moves) and I loved it!

The daydream usually went like this: I would be standing on a stage, silently waiting in the dark. Suddenly, the spotlight would come on me, making the sequins in my pink outfit shimmer ever so slightly. Then the music would begin. I could just picture the exact arm gestures I would do to the opening line, "When they gave me the bad news." Then I would do a half-turn on "I didn't know what do." I would flip my hands up on, "Was there something I should say?" and would of course fall to my knees on "or should I just kneel down and pray." Next I would leap . . .

"Cammie!" a voice called me from far off in the distance. (Cammie was my family nickname.)

My eyes were still closed as I made a joyful leap across the stage . . .

"Cammie!"

Now I was hunching my back and covering my face with my hands . . .

"Ashton Joy Daniels!"

Oh-oh. The music had been shut off and Dad had used my real, full name. I popped my eyes open and met his gaze in the rearview mirror of the car. "Yeah, Dad?"

"Will you be joining your sisters in school today? Or were you planning on coming back home with me?"

I giggled and unbuckled my seatbelt. "I guess I'll be joining my sisters."

"Good idea," Dad said, nodding. I watched the reflection of his eyes as they crinkled in a smile.

"Come *on*, Cammie!" Amber called to me from outside. I popped out of the car and hurried over to catch up with her. We were not identical twins, so we didn't look alike. People had no problem telling us apart. But they were always comparing us to one another anyway. Like, "Oh, she's the shy one and you're the more outgoing one." Or "She likes singing and you like dancing." My favorite one though was when someone called Amber "sugar and spice" and me "fire and ice." I liked the sound of that! Besides, I guess when you are sisters, people are always going to compare you to each other, whether or not you are twins.

"What happened? Did you forget something?" Amber wrinkled her forehead with the question.

"Yeah," I said. "I forgot to get out of the car!"

We followed Lena and Ansley as they walked through the opened front gates of our school, Roland Lake Christian Academy. The school was made up of three buildings. The main building was a big, old-fashioned mansion with white columns, and the two other brick buildings stood one on each side of it. The middle building actually *was* the middle school, and Ansley dashed off to meet her friends there. Lena veered off to the left, toward the high school. Amber and I headed right, to the elementary school building. But since students from all three schools were gathered together on the front lawn, we could all hear greetings to each one of us coming from different directions. Everyone knew us Daniels sisters because there were four of us and we were the only set of siblings that year who were attending classes in all three buildings.

"Ashton! Amber!" Our friends, Esperanza Harrison and June Harlow, called out to us.

We waved at them and stopped walking to allow the girls time to run over and join us. Rani (which is what we called Esperanza) and June were really best friends to each other, just like Amber and I were. But at school a lot of the time Rani was more like my best friend and June was Amber's. June had pale, reddish-blonde wispy hair that she usually wore in a simple ponytail, very light blue eyes, and eyelashes that were almost silver. Rani was practically her opposite. She had dark hair that she wore in two thick braids, super-dark eyebrows, super-dark eyelashes, and eyes that were almost black. Only by the time she reached me and came to a panting stop, I could see that her eyes were looking red and puffy today.

"What's wrong? Are you okay?" I asked.

Rani nodded as she caught her breath. Then she shook her head. "Yes—actually, no. I have bad news!"

"What happened?" Amber and I asked together.

"It's my dad," Rani said with a sob. "He got a promotion!"

I paused and exchanged glances with Amber. Wasn't a promotion supposed to be a good thing? "You mean . . . he's got a better, more important job?" I asked, squinting my eyes.

Rani nodded again.

Amber tilted her head. "Will he be paid more too?"

Rani nodded a third time.

I was definitely missing something. "So . . . what exactly *is* the problem?"

"Well, he didn't say 'yes' yet," Rani said. She started biting her fingernails.

"Why not?"

"Because the job's in London!" Rani blurted out, and she began to cry.

Amber immediately reached out to give her arm a squeeze. June patted Rani on the back. But I was still having trouble understanding.

"That's . . . terrible, Rani," I said. "I know you're going to miss him a lot. How long will he be away?"

"No! Don't you get it?" Rani accepted the packet of tissues

June handed to her. "I won't miss him. I'll be *with* him! We'll all have to move!"

I sucked in my breath. "Oooh. *You* won't be missing *him* . . . *we'll* be missing *you.*"

"Right!" Rani groaned. "And I'll miss all of you too!" A fresh batch of tears began to stream down her face.

"When is it supposed to happen?" Amber asked. Her voice was softer and higher than mine. "Like, by this summer?"

"That's the worst part," Rani said with a sniffle. "The job opened up unexpectedly. Dad needs to give them his answer in a week. And if he says 'yes' we'll probably be moving in two weeks!"

Amber and I gasped together.

"But there's more than two *months* left of school!" I shook my head. "It makes no sense to take you out now."

Rani shrugged. "It's supposed to be a really great job."

"No, no," I continued. "We can't let it happen. There's got to be some way to keep you here. I just know it." I patted her on the shoulder. "Don't worry. I'll think of something."

The four of us trudged up to the school, each quietly lost in her own thoughts. June had her head down. Amber was humming something to herself. Rani was still sniffling.

Think of a plan, I commanded myself. I lead the pack to the front doors of our building and toward the auditorium where our classes were lining up. It was when we were passing by the main office that it caught my eye. There was a colorful mini-poster on the bulletin board on the wall.

Do you sing? Do you dance? Are you a musician or comedian?
Don't hide your light under a bushel!

Sign up for
THE ROLAND LAKE
LOWER SCHOOL
Spring Talent Show!

"Hey, guys, take a look." I pointed to the brightly colored flyer. As my friends gathered around me to read it, I had a flashback to my daydream in the car. "Are any of you interested in signing up? How about you, Amber? You could sing."

Amber shook her head shyly. "In front of an audience? No way."

"I *would* dance," Rani said. Then she sagged her shoulders and sighed. "But this will take place around Easter. I'll probably be living in London by then!"

I frowned. "Don't say that! We can't let that happen!" I set my lips in a thin line. Then I felt an idea jump out of my brain like a warm slice of bread from a toaster. "Hey, maybe we can do a dance together," I said. "Something we have to practice a lot for, you know? Something you make sure to tell your parents you are looking forward to performing . . ."

"As you tell them how much you like your school and your friends . . ." Amber said, catching on.

Rani nodded with understanding. "I get it . . . ! You mean, being in the talent show might show them how much I want to stay so that maybe we don't go to London after all or at least not yet?"

"Exactly."

June clapped her hands and jumped up and down. "Great idea!"

"Oh, yes," Rani said breathlessly. "Oh, let's do it! Let's do it!"

"Okay, then. It's settled." I rubbed my chin in thought. Then, since Amber didn't take dance lessons with us, I pointed to June and Rani. "We three will do a dance together. A routine that needs at least three people to perform. Then your parents will see that we need you to stay, Rani. Okay?"

"Yes!" Rani and June chimed in at the same time.

Amber grinned at us, happy that we had a plan even though she couldn't really participate in it.

I smiled back at her. I just might be able to help my friend *and* get the chance to dance in a talent show. How great would that be? "Now let's get to class before Ms. Roderick gets mad," I said, leading the way to our classroom. I held my head up, trying to walk with a confidence that would make the others feel hopeful. But inside I was probably more nervous than all of them. *I really hope this plan works!* I thought. Besides my sisters, Rani was my best friend. I simply wasn't ready for her to leave. In fact, my stomach had been feeling sloshy and gross ever since she'd told us that she might move. I swallowed hard. *Have faith*, I told myself. *It will all work out.*

Chapter 2

Our teacher, Ms. Roderick, was a really nice lady who kept her blond hair short because (she told us) it was the best way to show off her earring collection. She seemed to have hundreds! I don't think I had ever seen the same pair twice. She explained that she had so many because once people found out how much she loved them, they always gave her earrings as gifts. Today she was wearing earrings that looked like tiny parrots perched on big, round swings dangling from her earlobes.

Ms. Roderick taught us a lot of subjects, like creative writing, math, history, and Bible studies. It was like she knew everything! But she didn't teach us science or art or gym. Those subjects needed special teachers, rooms, equipment, and storage.

So I was surprised when I saw Ms. Ericson, our art teacher, standing in the middle of our classroom. It was weird to see her, with her familiar red smock and cloud of grey hair, someplace other than her art studio. Sometimes I felt like she *lived* in her art studio. I imagined that she stayed there overnight. That after everyone was gone for the day, she put on pajamas, pulled out a sleeping bag, and slept on the floor, surrounded by paints, crayons, easels, and the artwork that covered the walls.

With a quiet chuckle at that silly idea, I glanced at Amber, who was getting ready to sit down next to me. She flashed me a look that asked, "What's Ms. Ericson doing here?" I sent her a look that said, "I was wondering the same thing!"

We wouldn't find out until after Ms. Roderick took attendance. And that took a while because Ms. Roderick got us all laughing when she called out our names using a parrot voice. "Amber Daniels? Brraaaak! Ashton Daniels? Brraaak!" Then she had to wait until everyone had calmed down before she could explain why Ms. Ericson was with us.

"You were supposed to have art a little later this morning," she said, "but the middle school needs to borrow our art studio today. A water pipe broke and flooded their art room and the seventh-grade class needs space for a project they've been working on. You'll have to have art here, instead."

"Yay!" Cheers went up around the room and kids clapped their hands. The teachers started handing out newspapers to spread out on top of our desks.

"We'll be using acrylic paints and special, oil-based markers today to paint and draw on these!" Ms. Ericson had a bucket full of flat, smooth rocks. Some were white, some were black, some were grey. "Do you have any idea what we'll be painting on them?"

I looked around at my fellow classmates. Our desks were arranged side-by-side in a horseshoe shape, with everyone facing the center of the classroom. This made it easy for all of us to see each other's faces. But judging by the blank or confused expressions I saw, no one seemed to have a clue what we would be painting.

Finally, someone called out, "Words?"

Then someone else guessed, "Animals?"

June raised her hand. "Whatever we want . . . ?"

Ms. Ericson laughed. "Those answers are all *sort of* correct. Actually, we will be painting these rocks with messages and images of kindness, welcome, and acceptance. They'll be perfect to use for your Matthew 25 project," she said.

Our Matthew 25 project was something the class had been working on all year. It was based on the Gospel of Matthew, chapter 25, verses 35, 36, and 40. In that Scripture, Jesus told his disciples some of the different ways that we could show love for our neighbor. We were learning how God's love in us drives us to love others and how that love for others was actually our love for God!

Ms. Roderick asked, "Can you guess which verse this art assignment will help you to live out?"

Since the verses happened to be written on banners hung near the ceiling all around the classroom, I swept my eyes over them for a quick reread.

The banner on my left had the words: *"For I was hungry and you gave me something to eat . . . I was thirsty and you gave me something to drink . . ."* The banner in front of me had the words, *"I was a stranger and you welcomed me . . . I was naked and you clothed me."* And the third said, *". . . I was sick and you visited me . . . I was in prison and you came to me."* And although I couldn't read the one on the banner behind me without turning around, I knew that the words were, *'Truly, I tell you, whatever you did for one of the least of these brothers and sisters of mine, you did for me."*

I read the words silently to myself, mouthing out the Scripture. Then I understood which verse we would be concentrating on that morning and my arm shot up.

"Yes, Ashton?"

"'I was a stranger and you welcomed me?'"

"Exactly!" Ms. Roderick beamed at me. "How did you figure that out?"

"Because," I said, hearing my own voice grow a little softer, "when my family and I first moved here, the people in our church welcomed us with a housewarming party. Some of them gave us painted rocks as presents. They're really pretty. We still have the rocks decorating the railing on our front porch."

"So the rocks worked, then? They helped you and your family to feel welcome?"

Amber and I both nodded.

Ms. Roderick clasped her hands together. "I'm glad to hear it. Because we're going to be doing just that for someone else. There will be a new student joining us on Monday," she announced. "Her name is Jasmyn Wright. And while it is unusual to have a new student this late in the school year, special circumstances in her life have brought her to us. You see, she has a medical condition that requires her to use a wheelchair. Because of this, her family has had to find a home that they could renovate to accommodate her growing needs. Now that it's ready, they plan on moving in this weekend."

As she spoke, Ms. Roderick walked around the inside of the horseshoe of desks. I watched as the parrots on her earrings swung back and forth. "While I am sure Jasmyn and her family are happy and excited that the big day is almost here, how do you think Jasmyn might feel about moving away from all of her friends? From everything familiar? How will she feel about having to learn a curriculum at a new school where she doesn't know anyone?"

I locked eyes with Rani. That's how it would be for her if she moved to London!

Rani's eyes were large and her face pale. "Scared," she said out loud.

"Yes," Ms. Roderick agreed.

"Worried," June added.

"Uncomfortable," someone else piped up.

"I'd hate it!" a boy named Andrew yelled out.

Ms. Roderick looked around the class approvingly. "I'm glad to see you can all put yourselves in her shoes. Now try to do that when you paint the rocks. Imagine what sort of message or picture you would like to see if you were in her position."

The two teachers handed out the rocks, paints, and markers, and soon we all got to work.

We each got one black rock and one white one. We were told that we should paint one to go on top of Jasmyn's desk for her to find on Monday. The other was supposed to be hidden someplace out in nature—like in a park or on a hiking trail or near a picnic spot—to be found by a stranger and hopefully make them smile and feel loved.

I turned the two rocks over in my hands. "Hmm," I said. "What should I paint?"

"I'm going to write 'You rock!'" Amber said. Dimples appeared on her cheeks as she enjoyed her little joke.

"Ooh. That's a good one for both Jasmyn or for a stranger to find," I admitted. I put down the black one and felt the weight of the white one in my palm for a minute. "What would I like to see if I were Jasmyn?" I mumbled to myself. Then I thought back to the rocks we had received when we first moved into town. *I guess if it were me,* I thought, *I'd like a rock with a pretty, cheerful picture on it.* Since my favorite color was pink, I picked a bright pink marker and began to draw a butterfly. As I added purple details and gold accents, I began hearing the Mallory Winston song from this morning in my head. Especially the chorus, which went:

I will sing praises to the Lord
For God is good.
God is good.
In the dark and in the light,
God is good.
I'll sing praises to the Lord
Throughout the day,
Throughout the night.
Because through everything and all
God is good.

And noticing that there was some room above the butterfly, I wrote the words "God is good." When I was done, I felt satisfied. "That's perfect," I told myself.

Next, I picked up the black rock. I tried to think of something else cool for Jasmyn, but my thoughts kept going back to Rani. So I ended up using bright blue paint to write "You belong here" on the rock. Then I took some white paint and added tiny white flowers all around the words and on the back of the rock. The blue and white looked great against the black background. Both of my rocks came out really pretty. *I wish I could give them both to Jasmyn,* I thought. *I hope she likes whichever one she ends up getting.*

When we were done, I helped clean up by going around the

room and collecting some of the newspapers to put them in a pile for recycling. When I headed back to my seat, I noticed that Ms. Roderick had pulled up a chair next to mine and was sitting in it. She looked like she was waiting to speak to me. Then she waved me over.

"Ashton," she said as I sat down. "This desk next to yours in the perfect spot for a student in a wheelchair, so I am going to put Jasmyn next to you, okay?"

"Okay."

"That means I'm going to need you to help her get accustomed to the way we do things around here. She might end up feeling a little lost having to catch up with everything. But if you act as sort of a "special buddy" to her and help her to settle in, I think it would be very beneficial for all of us. Would you be able to that?"

I nodded. "Of course." The truth was, I would have helped Jasmyn whether Ms. Roderick asked me to or not. I had been the "new girl" at school just a few months ago. And I had been so glad when June and Rani made friends with me and Amber right away. Knowing how that felt made me want to help someone else the same way. I also felt kind of proud that Ms. Roderick had singled me out to be the new girl's buddy. I wanted to do my best to not disappoint either of them.

When our class filed into the cafeteria at lunchtime, I noticed a table that was set up near the back. It was covered with a red tablecloth and there were balloons taped to the wall behind it. "Look!" I jumped up and down. "It's the sign-up table for the talent show. Let's go!"

I began to charge over when I noticed that Amber, June, and even Rani were all hanging back.

TALENT SHOW
Talent Show

"Are we really going to do this?" Rani began chewing her fingernails again. "I mean, what dance will we do for the show?"

"We can do the same routine we did at our dance recital last December," I said.

"But . . . won't we need more than three people for that?" June asked. We had danced with our entire dance class at our dance school's holiday recital.

"I don't think so." I tilted my head and thought about it for a moment. "No. We can make it work with just the three of us. Let's go!" I turned on my heel to lead them toward the table when Rani spoke again.

"But . . . we can't use the same music! Remember? Last time we danced to a Christmas song. It's almost Easter now."

"So, we'll pick a different song. No big deal. That's why we'll have to rehearse. Okay? Are we going to do this or not?" I looked back and forth from June's wrinkled forehead to Rani's wide eyes. "Have you changed your minds?" I put my hands on my hips and focused on June. "Do you want to let Rani go without a fight?"

"No, of course not. I just . . . I just want to be sure our dance will come out okay," June said. "I don't want us to mess up in front of everyone."

"I don't either," I said. "Believe me. But we have to try *something* to keep Rani here."

"You're right." June hung her head. Then, after taking a deep breath, she said, "Let's go."

Chapter 3

When we got to the table, a teacher from one of the lower grades whose name I didn't know raised her arms up high and cheered our arrival. "Woo-hoo! All right, ladies!" she said in a voice that was loud enough for everyone in the cafeteria to hear. "Going to sign up for the talent show? Yessss!"

For a minute I was afraid that June was going to turn around and run out the door, but she didn't. Maybe she figured with a welcome like that, there was no way she could back out now.

The teacher smiled at each of us in turn. "So, will you be four separate acts, one act together, or . . . ?" She arched one of her eyebrows over the frame of her reading glasses.

Amber giggled and shook her head. "Oh, I'm not signing up." She took a step backwards.

"Although she should," I said. "She can sing."

"Oh, come on," the teacher slid the sign-up sheet across the table so that it was closest to Amber. "Don't hide your light under a bushel," she told her.

"*We'll* sign up, anyway," I said, gesturing toward Rani, June, and myself. "We're going to do a dance together."

"Great!" The teacher handed me a pen to sign our names. "What do you girls call yourselves? Does your dance troupe have a name?"

"Oh." We hadn't thought of that. "No. Not yet." I jerked

my head in a confident nod to the others. "But we'll think of something."

"All right, then. Just know that things like your group names, song choices, and the themes of your dances all need to be okayed by the talent show committee before you can put on your performance. This handout explains all the rules." She passed out sheets of neon yellow copy paper from a stack. "Get these signed by your parents and you're all set. Any questions?"

We all shook our heads.

"Okay, then. I'll be here all period if you change your mind or suddenly think of something you want to ask me. I'm Ms. Greene." She waved good-bye as we headed for our regular table.

"Wow. We did it. We really did it," June said once we sat down. She stared down at the tabletop, not really seeing it. She seemed to be in shock. "We're going to be in the talent show!"

"When are we going to rehearse and stuff?" Rani asked in a panicked voice.

"I was thinking about that," I admitted. The wheels in my mind were always spinning. "And I thought maybe we can rehearse at my place after dance class on Saturday. How does that sound?"

"That sounds like a good idea," Rani said. "But please, let's make it my place instead."

I was hoping she'd say that. "That's a better idea," I said. "We want your parents to see how much fun you have with your friends and how important school here is to you." I rubbed my hands together. My plan was shaping up.

"You still need a name for the troupe," Amber said quietly.

"This is true. Anyone have any ideas?" I asked.

June began unwrapping a peanut butter and jelly sandwich. "How about the 'Say "No" to London Dance Troupe'?"

I slapped myself on the forehead and groaned. "I say 'no' to that name! We're not supposed to give away our plan like that!"

"Besides," Amber said, "London sounds really cool. I love English things. Like the Narnia book series. That's from England!"

Rani's eyes lit up. "Yeah! And *Alice in Wonderland* and *Peter Pan* and *Winnie-the-Pooh*! So many classic stories are English!"

I narrowed my eyes at my twin. What was she doing? She wasn't supposed to be making Rani *want* to move to London! I raised my voice to draw attention back to me. "How about a name that's closer to home? Something about staying home, maybe."

Amber closed her eyes and began repeating, "There's no place like home . . . there's no place like home . . ." Giggling, Rani and June joined in. "There's no place like home . . . there's no place like home . . . "

Better, I thought. *Kansas was way closer to home than London.* "That's it!" I jumped up from my seat.

The other girls were startled into silence and all stared at me wide-eyed.

"We can call ourselves . . . *The Ruby Slippers!* It's perfect because we're a dance troupe that's trying to prove that there is no place like home!"

June, Rani, and Amber all squealed in agreement.

I scrambled out of my seat. "Let's go tell Ms. Greene right now!"

By the end of the day our painted rocks were all dry and ready. And since it was Friday, the class decorated Jasmyn's desk with the rocks we chose to give her and took the ones we were supposed to leave somewhere outside for a stranger to find. I decided to leave the butterfly for Jasmyn and take the black one with the white flowers with me when Ms. Roderick looked at them and gasped.

"Oh, that's a perfect one for Jasmyn!" she said. She snatched up the black rock. "Did you know that jasmine flowers look like this? Tiny and white! They are small but mighty, because they have a very strong scent that's used in lots of perfumes."

"Oh," I said. I didn't know what else to say.

Ms. Roderick neatly placed the rock on top of Jasmyn's desk in the middle of all the others. She looked so pleased with it that I decided not to tell her that it wasn't the rock I had originally planned to leave there. Instead, I pocketed the pink butterfly one and shrugged to myself. Both rocks were pretty.

Then the bell for dismissal rang.

"Line up, everyone!" Ms. Roderick called out.

When our Aunt Sam picked us up and asked, "How was school today?" I didn't say "fine" (my usual answer). Instead, I actually *told* her (and Ansley and Lena). I told them all about Rani and how she might have to move away. Then I told them how she and June and I had all signed up for the talent show as part of a plan to keep her here. "We can't let Rani move," I said, with a strong shake of my head. "Not without a fight, anyway."

"Now, wait a minute," my aunt said in a gentle-but-firm tone. "The job sounds like it could be a good opportunity for her father—for the whole family! Why would you not want them to take advantage of something like that? Besides, Rani might end up loving London!"

I made a face. "Now you sound like Amber. I'm sure London is great and all that. It's just that I really don't want Rani to go." I looked down at my hands. "Besides, she doesn't want to go, either."

"That may be so," Aunt Sam said, turning the steering wheel left. "But maybe what you girls should be focusing on is just enjoying the whole talent show experience. I think it's great that you're going to dance together. It sounds like a fun, creative thing for best friends to do. And that's why you should do it: for fun. Not to . . . try to make other people do what you want."

My stomach sank. "What? What do you mean?"

"It sounds like you're all going to be more worried about whether your plan is working instead of having fun. What if, after all the time and effort you put into your plan, Esperanza has to move anyway? Decisions like moving to another country are not made easily. I'm sure Rani's parents want to do what's best for Rani. Do you want them to feel bad about moving to London?"

"No," I said. I twisted my mouth to the side and stared out the dusty window with a frown. I hadn't really thought of it that way. It was just that my mom had died unexpectedly over the summer. And it was very soon afterwards that my dad, my sisters, and I left our home, other members of our family, and all our friends behind to move to a new town and start a new life. I had lost so much already. Was I supposed to give up Rani too? It wasn't fair.

"Rani is my friend," I said, cutting through the quiet that had settled in the car. "I'm trying to help her. She wants me to help her. And isn't that what friends are for?"

"Of course, honey, I know," Aunt Sam said. Then, with a glance at Amber in the rearview mirror, she said, "And what about you, Kitty?" (She called her by her family nickname.) "Will you be in the talent show too? Singing, perhaps?"

Amber giggled. "No way. I don't want to sing in front of a lot of people."

"But you've sung in front of the family," Aunt Sam said. "You even let Cammie record you singing on video."

"That's true." Amber rolled the yellow talent show flyer into a tube shape and looked through it like a telescope. "But that was different. It was just her. And a teeny, tiny camera. Not a crowd of people all staring at me."

"Yeah," I chimed in. "She's used to being in front of a camera."

Amber and I liked to make little videos of ourselves, of each other, of our family—or anything! Sometimes we made up stories and filmed "movies" with scenes where we were pretending to be spies or detectives. Other times we filmed a pretend talk show we liked to call "The Cammie and Kitty Show" and recorded stuff like Lena singing and playing the guitar or Ansley baking her famous cinnamon rolls. It was because I liked to make videos so much that I was called "Cammie" by my family. It was short for "Camera Girl"—a nickname my mom had given me.

Ansley, who was riding in the backseat with me and Amber, spoke up. "You know, even though it can be scary to be on a stage in front of an audience, filming a video of yourself and putting it up on the internet can get you a much bigger audience! A huge one! Millions of people from all over the world can see you." She traced the shape of a globe in the air. "I think that's scarier."

Amber turned to her. "But I think videos are more fun. If you make a mistake, for instance, you can just do it over. You can't do that on a stage. When you mess up, everyone gets to see you do it!"

Lena, who was sitting in the front seat, slipped off her headphones to show us she was listening to the conversation. "Thank goodness for retakes! I needed them when I was filming *Above the Waters.* I was so nervous—especially in the beginning—I made plenty of mistakes. Even so, I have to say that there's something about performing on stage in front of a live audience that I think can actually help you make fewer mistakes than when you're in front of a camera. I remember when we were filming. Whenever the camera was on me, I would get a fluttery, nervous butterfly-like feeling in my stomach. But whenever I'm about to perform on stage, I get a fluttery, *excited* butterfly-like feeling in my stomach. They are similar, but different."

Amber sighed. "Yes, but when you sing, it's with Mallory Winston, or in a choir. In the talent show I would have to sing by myself. That's what's scariest!"

Aunt Sam pulled into our driveway. "Couldn't Lena sing with you? Like the way the two of you were singing in the car this morning?"

"Nooooo," the four of us said at the same time. I pointed to the flyer. "The talent show is for the lower school *only.*"

Aunt Sam clucked her tongue. "Of course. I wasn't thinking." She turned off the ignition. "Here we are! Home sweet home."

We all clambered out of the car and toward the sounds of barking dogs. Austin, our blue-nosed bully, and Zette, our aunt's French bulldog, were happy that we were home. I watched as my sisters entered the house and listened to them as they squealed over the dogs, but I lingered for a moment outside. I stopped to look at the painted rocks that were still decorating our front porch.

Some of the rocks were painted to look like cute ladybugs or owls. Some had emoji faces or patterned designs. A lot had inspiring words or phrases on them, like "God loves you" and "let's be friends" or "peace be with you." As I looked over all of them, I hunted for my favorite one. Finally, I found it. Rani had made it before even meeting me and becoming my friend. It was painted in sparkly pinks and purples and had the words "I hope you dance!" written across it. I decided to bring it to my room and keep it on my dresser for some inspiration. I slipped it into my skirt pocket and heard a soft "click" sound when it knocked into the butterfly rock that was still there.

"I hope you dance, too, Rani," I said under my breath as I opened the front door. "I hope we *both* dance."

Chapter 4

Dad, Aunt Sam, Lena, Amber, and I were all seated around the dinner table, ready to have some spaghetti and meatballs, but we couldn't. One of us was missing.

"Ansley! We're waiting!" Dad called for about the third time.

"Okay, okay!" Ansley yelled from her room (also for about the third time). "I'm coming, I'm coming!" This time we could hear her actual footsteps thumping down the stairs.

When she appeared in the kitchen, she had a faraway look in her eyes and a unicorn horn strapped to her forehead.

"You want to wash your hands?" Dad asked her as his gaze drifted up to her forehead.

"What? Oh!" Ansley noticed his gaze and her hands flew up to the horn. Then she laughed as she took it off. "I was doing math!" she explained as she went to the kitchen sink to wash her hands.

"That still doesn't . . ." Lena drifted off.

"I was starting on my math homework." Ansley slipped into her seat at the table. "I didn't want to forget anything we learned in class today. We have a test on Monday," she explained, "and I want to keep it all fresh in my mind over the weekend so that I can do well on it."

I shot a glance over at the unicorn headband she had laid

down on the back of the couch behind her chair. "And . . . unicorns are good at math?"

Ansley laughed. "I needed to concentrate. So, I looked for something to help me focus. Like a thinking cap. Then I found that! It was perfect. Like an antenna to grab all the smarts from the air and get it into my brain!"

We all giggled at that. Ansley loved all things unicorn, so the horn was a perfect thinking cap for her.

"Do you think it worked?" Dad smiled at her.

"Yup!" Ansley smiled back. "But we'll know for sure after the test on Monday."

Dad thumped her on the back. "You've worked really hard at keeping your math grade up this year," he said warmly. "I'm very proud of you. I'm sure you'll do well on your test." Then he folded his hands together. "Okay, ladies. It's time to give thanks to God."

We all bowed our heads.

"Heavenly Father, we thank you for providing us with the blessing of this delicious meal that Aunt Sam has prepared for us. May it nourish us body and spirit in Your Name." Dad looked at all of us seated at the table. "Would anyone else us like to add their thanks?"

"I will," I said. I closed my eyes. "And thank you, God, for my friendship with Rani and for helping us with the talent show idea. Amen." When I opened my eyes, my sisters had started eating. Dad, though, was looking at me questioningly.

"What's all this about Rani and a talent show?" he asked. He started twirling spaghetti around his fork.

I told him the story. "Can we rehearse at Rani's after dance class tomorrow? Can we? Pleeease?" I asked when I was done explaining.

"Yes, you may, but first I want to understand a little bit more about your plan," Dad said. I saw him flicker a look at Aunt Sam for half a second. I wondered if she had told him about our conversation in the car. "I don't mind your being in the talent show. In fact, I think it sounds great. But I'm a little worried about how you're going to feel about it if your plan doesn't work."

I sighed. Why didn't he or Aunt Sam have faith in the plan? "I think it will work, though, Dad. I mean, you weren't there. You didn't see the way that poster popped up just when I needed a plan to keep Rani here. It has to be more than a coincidence. It's like God wants her to stay too. He must be helping us."

"God is always helping us," Dad said. "But His ways are not like our ways."

"What do you mean?" I asked, nibbling on a meatball.

"It says so in the Bible." Dad began looking up the Scripture verse on his phone. He didn't usually like any of us using a phone at the table but using it to look up Bible verses was always okay. "Here it is. In Isaiah, chapter 55, verses 8–9." He cleared his throat then read, "'For my thoughts are not your thoughts, neither are your ways my ways,' declares the Lord. 'As the heavens are higher than the earth, so are my ways higher than your ways and my thoughts than your thoughts.'"

"Um, okay," I said. I wasn't sure what he was trying to tell me.

Dad reached out and laid a hand on my arm. "All I am saying is that we don't always know what God is planning for us. We can try to cooperate with his plans, though, especially by praying that His will be done in our lives. It's just that sometimes what *He* wants for us is not always what *we* want for us. That's why we pray for His help to understand or at least accept when things don't go the way we want them to. It means having faith that His plan is better—His plan is *best*—even if we can't see it at first. Okay?"

"Okay," I said. I truly believed everything Dad said. But I also believed that my plan *was* God's plan in this particular situation. I decided not to talk about it anymore. Instead, I mentioned that there was going to be a new girl in my class starting next week and how Ms. Roderick had asked me to be her special buddy and show her how things are done at school. "Her name is Jasmyn. She's in a wheelchair."

"Oh, yes. I heard about the Wright family moving into town. In fact, they should be in church this Sunday. So, you might get to meet Jasmyn before Monday."

That meant I could end up meeting the new girl before most of the other kids in my class. I wriggled in my chair. "That would be cool!"

That night, after changing into my owl pajamas, I laid out the two painted rocks side-by-side on my bedspread. Then I kneeled for a short prayer. "God, please show me how to help Rani. Also, please help her family figure out what's best to do about the job offer." Then, remembering what my dad had said earlier, I added, "Your ways above my ways. Amen."

As Amber began climbing the ladder to the bunk bed over mine, I plumped up my pillow, snuggled under my blanket, and smiled. I felt sure that with God in charge, Rani's situation would work out just right. I was so sure, in fact, that I was already dancing in my dreams before Amber reached the top rung of the ladder.

The next morning Aunt Sam dropped me off at Tambourine Studios, my dance school. It was in the center of town and had two floors of practice rooms with springy wood floors, pink walls, and lots of mirrors. They taught all kinds of dance there: ballet, jazz, tap, hip-hop, and of course, my favorite, lyrical dance. When I first started going there, I wondered about the school's unusual name. It was my dance teacher, Ms. Mandy, who told me that it came from the Bible. She said that people in the Bible like King David or Miriam (the sister of Moses), were said to be dancing to tambourine music when they praised God. "And that's what we like to do here," Ms. Mandy said. "Praise God!"

With a wave to Aunt Sam, I jumped out of the car, ran through the front door, and made a beeline for the locker room. Finding Rani and June already there, I pounced. "So?" I panted. "Did you tell your parents about the talent show, Rani? What did they say?"

"Well," Rani pulled her hair back in a ponytail, "they said I could enter . . ."

My heart soared. "That's good news!" I nodded at June, who was jumping up and down in place.

". . . because," Rani continued, not smiling, "I should just keep doing everything as usual until they have made their decision."

I took a deep breath but refused to be discouraged. "It's still good . . . it's still good. Then it's okay if we go over to your place and practice later?"

"Yup." Rani flashed me a thumbs-up. "It's all set!"

I pumped a fist in the air. "Yessss!"

During that afternoon's class, Ms. Mandy decided to teach us some new moves. And while I usually liked learning new moves, putting them together in a sequence usually took me a little time. And it was even harder than usual for me to concentrate because I had so many other things going on in my mind.

Ms. Mandy, who was young and was wearing her long curly hair in a ponytail, looked over her shoulder to smile at me. "Having some trouble with the choreography today, Ashton?"

I felt a little hot around my neck and cheeks. "Kind of," I admitted. I tried not to notice how well Mariska Murphy and Quinn Kozlowski were doing. They had learned the new steps easily—which was typical, really. They were the two best dancers in class. *They both go to Roland Lake, too,* I remembered. *I wonder if they entered the talent show . . .*

When class was over, Rani, June, and I changed quickly. As I pulled on my red sweater, I remembered that it was the same sweater I had worn for our Christmas dance recital. *Now how did that dance go again?* I wondered to myself. I raised my hands above my head and began to dance what I could remember of the beginning. "It's harder without the music," I said to Rani and June. "Which move did we do first? Was it this move?" I asked. "Or did we—"

"What are you doing?"

I stopped mid-spin to see Mariska and Quinn watching us.

Mariska had asked the question, but Quinn followed it up with a question of her own. "Isn't that the routine we did at the Christmas recital?"

"Yeah," I said, my hands still arched over my head. "I'm trying to remember it."

June added, "We're going to perform it at the talent show."

I winced, but both Mariska's and Quinn's faces lit up. "You're all going to be in the talent show?" Mariska clasped her hands together. "How cool!"

"The three of you together, right?" Quinn wrinkled her nose. "But don't you need more people for that dance?"

"No. I'm sure we can figure out a way to make it work," I said. I didn't really want to change too much of the choreography if I could help it. I needed to remember all of it for the talent show.

"You know," Mariska said, standing taller and taller before our eyes, "you wouldn't have to change it much—or at all—with a couple more dancers."

"What?" Rani blinked hard.

Quinn's smile looked sneaky. "In fact, it would work perfectly with five people."

I lowered my arms.

"Are you saying . . . what I *think* you're saying?" Rani asked hesitantly.

Mariska finally just spat it out. "Can we join your act?" She held her breath.

"Yes!" Rani and June squealed back at once.

"Wait a minute, wait a minute," I said. I didn't want to be difficult, but the talent show had been my idea. I was basically the leader of the group, and now suddenly June and Rani were making decisions about our dance troupe without me.

I decided to explain to Mariska and Quinn why it might not be such a good idea that they join us. "Actually, the three of us are already signed up as The Ruby Slippers. They have all of our names and everything. It might be too late to add anyone to the act."

"Nah," Mariska said, taking her brown hair down from its bun. It tumbled down as a fluffy bob that just reached her shoulders. "I'm sure there won't be a problem adding our names to the act."

"I love the name The Ruby Slippers!" Quinn said. She took down her bun too. But her brown hair was longer and wavy. Then she borrowed Mariska's hair tie and gave herself two low ponytails to look like Dorothy in the movie *The Wizard of Oz*. "There's no place like home . . ." she said. "There's no place like home!"

I shot a sidelong glance at Rani and June. "Yeah. That's *exactly* it. In fact, we're doing this dance for a kind of personal, private reason."

Quinn frowned and crossed her arms. "Oh. I get it. You just don't want us."

"No! That's not it!" I tried to figure out a better way to say what I meant.

Rani nudged me. "It's okay," she said. "They can join us."

June nodded excitedly. "It's okay with me too."

Mariska lifted her teal-colored dance bag and threw it over her shoulder. "But if Ashton doesn't want us, maybe Quinn and I can sign up for the talent show ourselves."

"And *we* remember the choreography from the Christmas recital," Quinn said with a pout.

I felt the blood drain from my face. We couldn't have two dance troupes performing the same dance in the same talent show! Especially if one of the performances ended up being better than the other! *I really would not like it if their dance came out better than ours,* I thought. *Especially since it was our idea in the first place.*

"Don't be silly," I said aloud. "Nobody will want to see the same dance twice that evening. I just meant that Rani, June, and I are all friends. We're having rehearsals at our houses and stuff. In fact, we're all going to Rani's house after this. To come along, wouldn't you need permis—?"

But I didn't get to finish. Mariska and Quinn were already on either side of Rani. They were tugging at her sleeves and begging, "Oooh! Can we come? Can we come?"

Rani looked a little flustered, but she nodded and said, "Sure. I mean, if your parents say it's okay."

"Great! I'm going to ask my mom right now!" Mariska said. "Come on, Quinn!"

The two girls dashed out of the room, leaving me, Rani, and June to just stand around and stare at one another in silence.

Finally, Rani said in a slightly strained voice, "Won't it be cool having Mariska and Quinn with us?"

"Yeah!" June enthusiastically agreed.

I bent down to stuff my dance clothes into my purple gym bag. But also to hide the doubtful expression on my face. I didn't want to say it, because I didn't want to hurt her feelings or make her worry, but . . . somehow, I got the feeling that having Mariska and Quinn with us wasn't going to turn out as "cool" as Rani thought it would.

Chapter 5

Sadly, I was right.

In the beginning, though, it was fine. Great, even. When the five of us girls arrived at Rani's house, we all got to sit at a picnic table in her backyard and joke around while her mom got us lunch. Then we stuffed our faces. I was so hungry! I gobbled up my delicious hamburger so fast that Mrs. Harrison thought she had forgotten to make me one, so she made me another. That made me laugh!

When we were done eating, Mrs. Harrison told us we could practice in the family room. That sounded like a good idea to me.

Then we had to pick a song. That's when all the problems began.

I thought about suggesting "God Is Good" since I was always daydreaming a dance to it. But that was just it. I had a special dance in my head for that song. I didn't want us to use that song while using the Christmas recital choreography. And I didn't want to teach the girls *my* choreography. For one thing, I didn't think we had the time. For another, I kind of wanted to keep dreaming about that dance instead of actually doing it. At least for a little while longer.

Besides, everyone already knew the dance we did at Christmas. We just had to remind ourselves how it went and practice a version that worked for the five of us.

"Hmmm. Why don't we use the song "Let It Be Done?" I suggested. I began to dance and sing at the same time to show them how the music and moves could work together. I thought they were a perfect fit.

"See?" I said. I thought the decision was made.

But Mariska waved her hand. "Nah. I don't like that song so much. How about "Little Faith?"

"Ooh, yeah, I like that song!" Rani said.

I crossed my arms. I knew that Rani happened to love "Let It Be Done." It was one of her favorite songs. But she didn't say so when I suggested it. I watched Rani as she eagerly called up "Little Faith" on her music player and pressed play. When the first few notes of the song began, I found myself uncrossing my arms. I couldn't help it. I also really liked the song, even though I kind of didn't want to admit it. But then I watched Mariska and Rani try to dance to it using the Christmas choreography. I crossed my arms again and said, "Nope." I shook my head. "That's not working."

"Wait, wait!" Mariska said. "We can make it work! Watch. We'll just change this move from *one* turn to *two* turns. And instead of leaping here, we'll sort of stomp slowly . . ."

"You're making up new choreography," I said, still shaking my head.

"So?" Mariska said. "We can make it work." She gestured at June, Rani, and Quinn. "Go ahead, try it."

I watched as the girls tried the new moves to the music. They didn't seem able to get the hang of the stomping moves because Mariska kept changing her mind about how it should be done.

When I clucked my tongue, Rani looked at me. "We can do it," she insisted. "Come on, Ashton. Why don't you try?"

"Mariska," I said, starting to feel frustrated. "You said we wouldn't have to change any of the moves if you and Quinn could join us. It's only been five minutes and you're changing everything already!"

Mariska turned a little red. "Oh, I did say that, didn't I? Okay, then, let's not change anything. But let's dance it faster so that it can go more to the music. Like this."

She started dancing double-time. It looked rushed and a little sloppy.

"This song is way faster than the one we used at Christmas," I pointed out. "Listen to it! If we dance as fast you are asking us to, we're going run out of moves before the song is half over!"

"Oh," June said. "That wouldn't be good."

Mariska huffed. "Fine. Let's choose something else."

We named song after song. But it seemed that every song Mariska chose I didn't like, and every song I chose she didn't like.

"We should let Rani choose," I said.

Rani held up her hands in surrender. "Oh, no. I can't choose. I don't care. Any song you guys want is fine with me."

"That's the problem. We can't seem to decide." I grit my teeth. "Our rehearsal time is almost over, and we still haven't picked a song, yet." This wasn't good at all.

"Well, then maybe we should go over something else," Mariska said. "Like costumes!"

"What do you mean?"

"We haven't discussed costumes yet," Mariska said. "I was thinking tulle skirts would look really pretty."

I gagged. "Tulle skirts? Like ballerinas? This isn't ballet."

"We can add some ballet moves," Mariska said, raising her voice a little.

"No." I wrinkled my nose. "We're not dancing ballet. Besides," I rose my voice to match hers, "we already agreed no more new moves!"

Apparently, our voices were getting a little loud, because Mrs. Harrison came in the room just then to check on us and make sure everything was okay.

"Everything's fine," we all chimed in together.

"We're just discussing costumes," I said. "Why don't we all just wear black leotards and shorts or something, like we do at Tambourine? That way no one has to buy anything, but we can still match."

"That sounds . . . practical." Mrs. Harrison nodded at me.

"But boooorrrrrring," Mariska bellowed. "We should at least have something extra. Like red shoes, or something. We *are* called The Ruby Slippers!"

June drummed her fingertips against one another. "Oooh. I like that idea!"

"Shoes can be expensive, though," Rani said. Then she slowly turned to look at her mother with big, puppy dog eyes.

Mrs. Harrison, who worked for a shoe company, chuckled. "I'm sure I can find inexpensive dance slippers somehow." She ran a hand down Rani's ponytail lovingly.

"Oh, thank you!" Rani gave her mother a squeeze and exchanged secret glances with me. Could it be her mother was on our side? The London decision was supposed to be made in *one* week, but the talent show was in *three*! If she was willing to buy new dance slippers for the talent show, it sounded like she intended for Rani to be in the show.

Feeling a glimmer of hope rise within me, I turned to address all the girls. "Okay," I said. "So, it's settled. We wear our black leotards and shorts and—probably—red slippers. But we still have to pick a song!"

"Can I help?" Mrs. Harrison gestured at the sofa. "What seems to be the problem?"

The five of us squeezed ourselves into the overstuffed, flowered couch and explained our dilemma.

"I think I can settle this matter," Mrs. Harrison said getting up from the chair she'd been sitting on while listening to us. "I suggest that you each pick a song. Then we'll write their titles down on strips of paper." She reached for a notepad that was on the coffee table. "Then I'll fold them up, throw them in this bowl . . ." she pointed to a crystal decoration on the coffee table, ". . . and mix them up. "Then I will close my eyes and pull one of the strips out. Whatever song I choose will be the one. Does that sound fair?"

Rani, June, Mariska, Quinn, and I all agreed. We even all took turns mixing the strips in the bowl ourselves (just to make sure it was *really* mixed) before Mrs. Harrison mixed it for one final time herself.

Turning her head and closing her eyes, she felt around the bowl until she pulled out one of the folded strips. "And the song will be . . ." She pulled down her reading glasses from their perch on the top of her head. 'With You Always!'" She searched our faces. When she saw Quinn's light up, she knew it had been her choice.

Quinn did a little victory dance around the coffee table. The rest of us clapped good-naturedly. It was a good song, and I could see the dance moves working to the music.

The sound of a car horn honking outside let us know that rehearsal time was over.

"That's my dad," Mariska said. "When can we come here to rehearse again?"

Rehearse again? I thought. *We hadn't really rehearsed at all! More like argued about music and costumes.*

"How about Monday after school?" Mrs. Harrison suggested. "You can't on Wednesday because you have regular dance at Tambourine then."

"Monday. Okay! I'll ask my dad. Come on, Quinn, you're coming with me!" And with that, Mariska and Quinn left, almost skipping out of the room.

"I like them!" Rani said happily, throwing herself down on the couch in the space Mariska had left empty.

"Me, too!" June said, flopping down next to Rani, where Quinn had been. "Don't you?" she asked me.

I got up from the couch. "Yeah," I said, less enthusiastically. I wasn't lying. I liked Mariska and Quinn fine, really. What I didn't like was constantly getting into disagreements with Mariska about what our performance should be like. I wasn't sure I liked the idea of there being five Ruby Slippers either. But the dance was really for Rani's sake, and she wanted them there. *I guess if she's happy, I'm happy,* I thought. *And since Mariska and I seemed to have settled things, we shouldn't have any more problems from now on.*

But when Aunt Sam picked me up and asked me how things had gone, I couldn't help but sigh. "Bad," I exhaled. "I think there are too many of us in the group. Too many opinions. We didn't get far at all. But it's what Rani wants, so . . ." I shrugged my shoulders and turned to stare out the window.

Aunt Sam looked thoughtfully out at the road. "It is good to learn to collaborate with others. You know, to work in a group where everyone gets to participate. And to learn how to compromise."

"I know," I said tiredly. "But sometimes for things to work—even in a group—there needs to be a leader who's in charge."

Aunt Sam said, "You know what? I agree with you one hundred percent. But aren't you the leader?"

"I thought I was," I grumbled. "But Mariska kept trying to take over."

Aunt Sam pulled into the parking lot of a nearby mall. "Well, maybe she should be the leader if she can get the girls to listen to her."

"What?" I was shocked that Aunt Sam seemed to be on her side. "No! With Mariska leading we waste too much time on everything but the actual dance." I sighed. "If all of our rehearsals go like that, we'll end up not even getting the chance to perform."

"Well, then, it sounds like you'll have to figure out what to do so that doesn't happen." My aunt shut off the engine and pulled the key out of the ignition. "Unless you want to quit."

My heart thumped a few extra hard beats at the sound of the word "quit."

"No way," I said. "I can't quit. This is for Rani. So she can stay. I couldn't do that!"

"I didn't think so." Aunt Sam reached over and gave me a few pats on the shoulder. "It looks like you'll have to figure out how to be the leader then. And let me give you a big hint—the best leaders lead by example. That's what Jesus did. He not only told people how to live their lives, he showed them by living that kind of life."

"Hmmm," I said. "So, you're saying I need to *be* the kind of dancer I want the others to be?"

"Exactly. Instead of arguing with them or whining about how they are not taking things seriously, *show* them how to take things seriously. Do you think you can do that?"

"I can try," I said, even though I wasn't sure how.

"I know you can do it." Aunt Sam pointed at the grocery store. "I need to pick up some things before heading back." She opened the door on her side. "Maybe I'll buy some ingredients to make a cake."

I widened my eyes. "Your famous, amazing, wonderful, chocolate cake?"

"That's the one," Aunt Sam said. She turned to smile at me through the car window.

It sounds like this day is going to end better than it began, I thought, and I hopped out of the car.

Later that afternoon, when I was back home, I helped my aunt unpack the groceries. We had just finished when I heard the strains of "God is Good" coming from upstairs. Only instead of Mallory Winston, it was being sung by Lena and Amber. I scrambled for my phone and turned on the camera. Then I slowly walked up the stairs, filming my every step as I followed the sound of their voices. Finally, I found them in the family room on the top floor. As I entered, I found them both sitting on one side of the big, comfy, sectional couch. Lena was giving Amber another harmonizing lesson.

Still filming (but not saying a word) I tip-toed over to the other section of the sofa and sat down. And as I continued to record, I found myself closing my eyes to imagine my dance. But each time I did, I forced myself to pop my eyes open so I didn't mess up my recording. But when Lena made the two of them sing the second stanza another time, I put my phone down and began to dance. I couldn't help it. I had some good moves in my head that I just knew would go well with the words. Which were:

I thought: what would Mommy do?
What would she tell me to do?
When things didn't go my way?
She'd say don't give in to fear.
Have faith, trust in Him,
Even when you don't feel Him, Sweetie,
He is working even when you don't see Him.
And praise Him each and every day.
And so,
I'll trust and praise Him anyway!

As I danced, I noticed Lena and Amber look at me, but they didn't stop singing. They just continued to sing along as I danced. It was a little awkward for me sometimes because there wasn't enough space in the room for some of my moves. But it felt good to dance what I had seen in my head for so long. Plus, it was to a song I loved, and my sisters sounded really good together.

When it was over, we clapped for each other and bowed at one another. Then I sat back down on the other end of the couch.

"That was really good, Cammie," Lena said. I could tell she meant it.

But when she called me "Cammie" I suddenly remembered my phone was still recording. I snatched it up. "Oh," I groaned as I played it back. "I have some good footage of the ceiling."

"Well, I have some good footage of *you*," Amber said. She showed me she had taken some video of me dancing. I hadn't noticed since I had been concentrating on my choreography (and on not bumping into anything).

"Maybe you can edit them together into one recording," Lena said, looking down at both of our phones.

"That's true," Amber and I said at the same time. I really liked that idea. Then I had another idea.

"Hey, don't we have a recording of the Christmas recital in the computer somewhere?" I asked my sisters.

"Aunt Sam recorded it," Amber said, tapping her chin with her pointer finger. "Let's ask her if she downloaded it."

Soon Aunt Sam stuck a flash drive into the TV in the family room, and we watched as the video of my performance with my dance class filled the screen. I scrutinized every second of it. When it was over, I played it again and again, practicing along with it for a while. As I did this, little by little the whole dance came back to me. Then, turning the volume all the way down on the video, but playing the song "With You Always" on my phone, I danced and watched and listened *again,* trying to figure out how to make the dance work with the song Quinn had chosen.

At different points during my practice, each of my sisters walked into the room.

First it was Lena, but all she did was tip-toe into the room, whisper "sorry," grab her guitar, and leave.

Next it was Ansley. She stood just inside the room and watched me for a few minutes.

"What?" I asked, not stopping. "Did you need something?"

Ansley, who had her hands behind her back, suddenly held

out her unicorn horn headband to me. "I was going to ask if *you* needed *this*," she said, "because you're studying, too, aren't you? Like me for my math test. But it looks to me like you're pretty focused and don't need it at all."

I smiled and shook my head. "No, I don't," I said a little breathlessly. "But thanks!"

Ansley flashed me a thumbs-up and skipped out of the room.

Finally, Amber came in. By that time, I was feeling confident enough with the dance that I could take a break. Panting, I threw myself on the couch and stuck out my tongue, reminding myself of Zette (Aunt Sam's little French Bulldog) on a hot day.

Amber lingered in the doorway and looked from me to the computer and back to me again. "You done?"

I sat up and started sniffing the air. "Mmmm," I said. Suddenly my stomach rumbled loudly.

Amber glanced at my stomach. "I came to say that dinner's ready," she said.

I sniffed the air again. "That's not all that's ready!" I said, taking in the sweet smell that had made its way all the way to the top floor. "So is Aunt Sam's Extra-Special Delicious Double Chocolate Cake!"

"Yup!" Amber said. "Coming?"

I jumped off the couch. "Right behind you!" I grinned and followed my sister out of the room.

Chapter 6

The next morning, I got up before Amber. As I headed to the bathroom to brush my teeth, I caught sight of the two framed Scripture verses that hung on the wall opposite our beds. They were presents from Dad when we first moved into our new house. He had taken four Bible verses that Mom had written in a prayer journal, got them enlarged and framed, and gifted one to each one of us girls. Each verse was different. Mine said:

> Have I not commanded you? Be strong and courageous. Do not be afraid; do not be discouraged, for the Lord your God will be with you wherever you go.
>
> Joshua 1:9

Reading it every morning had become my daily ritual. It was a pick-me-up. Every time I read it, it seemed to make me stand straighter and to make my sleepy, droopy eyes pop open. I especially liked the way it reminded me that God was always, always with me. It made me feel safe and loved.

Feeling a little refreshed before I even brushed my teeth, I squeezed some minty green toothpaste onto my pink toothbrush. Then I noticed something from out of the corner of my eye. It was a pattern of white flowers that decorated the label of the liquid hand soap that stood on the sink. *Are those jasmine flowers?* I wondered. *Speaking of . . . will I get to meet Jasmyn today at church?* I hoped so.

When I got downstairs, I saw Aunt Sam starting to cook in the kitchen. It also looked like my dad was already in his office. But none of my other sisters were up. So, after wondering what to do, I found myself going up to the playroom and turning on the computer. I practiced the Christmas routine again. *Our next rehearsal needs to be a lot better than our first one,* I thought determinedly. *And as the leader of our group, I'll have to make sure it is.*

I practiced for about fifteen minutes—until the smell of bacon told me it was time to stop!

Later that morning, as we pulled up to a parking space in front of our church, I noticed an unfamiliar van parked not too far away. A man and woman I did not know had opened a side door and set up a small ramp next to the opening. Then a girl about my age with straight, blond hair, emerged from inside the van. She was sitting in a motorized wheelchair and propelling it forward with a control that looked like a joystick. I watched as slowly but surely she piloted her chair down the ramp and onto the asphalt. Then, smiling widely, she did a little spin—like a pirouette—with the chair.

I gasped. "That must be Jasmyn!" I shouted to everyone in the car. "Can I go see her, Dad? She's going to sit next to me in school tomorrow!"

"Me, too!" Amber said. "I want to meet her."

Lena turned her head to look out the side window. "She looks interesting."

Ansley stretched her neck to see past me and Amber. "Let's all go. She should meet all the Daniels sisters."

"Now hold up," Dad said. "You can't all go running over to her out of nowhere. She might feel a little overwhelmed being rushed at by four strangers, no matter how friendly."

"Yeah," I said. "It's 'welcome the stranger.' Not 'scare the stranger.'" I chuckled at my own joke. "Besides it was my idea first."

"Let Cammie and Kitty go first," Dad told Ansley and Lena. "You can introduce yourselves a little later."

Amber and I exchanged eager glances as we scrambled out after Lena and Ansley. But I wanted to be the one to meet her first since I was supposed to be her special buddy. So, the minute I got out, I shot ahead to make sure that I got there ahead of Amber. Hearing our hurried steps, the man, the woman, and the girl in the wheelchair all looked over to watch us as we ran over to them.

"Hi!" I waved as I came to a stop. "I'm Ashton Daniels. This is my sister, Amber." I introduced us to the grown-ups. Then I spoke directly to the girl. "We're in your class. I mean, you are Jasmyn, right?"

Jasmyn giggled. "Yes, I'm Jasmyn." Her eyes sparkled behind her glasses.

"I've never seen orange eyeglass frames before," I told her. "Those are cool."

She pointed to her chair. "Thanks. They match my wheels."

She wasn't kidding. Her powerchair was trimmed with orange highlights. "Cool," I said again.

"Yeah, cool." Amber nodded.

I gestured behind us. "That's my dad, my aunt, and my sisters. Can they say 'hi' too?"

Soon the adults were speaking to each other and my sisters

and I were walking alongside Jasmyn as we all headed into church together.

"We'll show you where to go," Lena assured her.

When we did, I suddenly became very aware of anything on the ground—like rocks or bumps and things—that might give her wheelchair a problem. I was glad to find that the ground was paved and mostly flat around the church. And the church itself (which was a bunch of new, white buildings clustered together) was easy for a wheelchair to enter. There were no stairs or anything. She could "drive" straight in. I felt very relieved about that and proud of my church for making it easy for people on wheels. But I was a little surprised at myself for not ever noticing before how easy or hard it might be for a person in a wheelchair to get around the church. I had seen people in wheelchairs at our services before. I had just never thought about how they had been able to get there in the first place.

A little while later, Jasmyn, Amber, and I were all settled in our Sunday school classroom. Ms. Candace, our teacher, told me to show Jasmyn what we had been working on.

I bent over a bin that had my name written on it (on a piece of duct tape), reached in, and took out my project. It was a square piece of open weave canvas. I unrolled it to show a half-finished work of art made of stitches of special colored threads. "We're working on needlepoint," I said. "Our group is doing pictures that represent gifts of the Holy Spirit. I have 'Patience.' See?" I showed her the picture that I was working on. There was an image of a girl smiling down at a seedling sprouting out of the earth.

"I have 'Love,'" Amber said. Her needlepoint was a picture of a child hugging a puppy.

DIAMOND
BOARD
1st =
2nd =
3rd =
cottons

"Once they're done, we're going to have them made into pillowcases and sell them at the church fair to raise money for the new playroom."

"And if they don't sell," Amber said, "we're going to use them to decorate the new playroom."

"Would you like to try?" Ms. Candace asked. "I have other patterns left. More fruit of the spirit. Or pictures of nature. What would you like?"

Jasmyn pointed to a pattern that showed a sunflower and a beaming sun. "'Joy'!" she said, choosing another fruit of the spirit. "I think I can use some orange in this," she explained to me in a whisper. I had made sure to use my favorite color on the little girl's pink dress in my picture, so I understood completely.

"Do you need me to show you how to make any stitches?" I asked. "There are like, literally a thousand different kinds. We're just using a half-cross stitch."

"Oh, I know how to needlepoint," Jasmyn told me. "I know how to knit and crochet too. I love this stuff." She reached out and stroked the picture I was working on. "Yours is coming out so great."

"Yeah," I said. "But look at this." I flipped it over. The back of it was a messy jumble of threads. "It's a disaster."

"It's not a disaster," Jasmyn said soothingly. "They always look like that in the back. Besides, you know what the pastor in my old church told me and my parents? He said that God is making beautiful needlepoint pictures with our lives. He can see them on his side, but we can only see the messy part on our side. But when we are in heaven with him, He will show us the beautiful pictures our lives made." Jasmyn flipped my canvas back and forth, to look at the front and back and front again. "We just have to have faith that He knows what He's doing." She handed me back the canvas.

I studied the picture I had been working on. "And praise Him," I said. Suddenly the lyrics to "God is Good" began playing in my head.

Then, as if she could read my mind, Jasmyn said, "Yeah, exactly. It's like that song that's on the radio. You know, the one that goes, 'I will sing praises to the Lord . . .'"

". . . throughout the day, throughout the night, because through everything and all God is good? I *love* that song!" I almost shouted.

"Me too!" Amber joined it. "I was just singing it with Lena the other day."

"Lena and Amber can really sing!" I fumbled for my phone. "Wait," I said. "I recorded some of it." I quickly found the video and began to play it for Jasmyn.

As she listened, Jasmyn's eyes opened wider and wider. "Wow, you do sound good," she told Amber seriously.

"Thanks!" Amber looked pleased.

"I told her she should enter the talent show our school is having. But she's too nervous," I said.

Amber said nothing. She just pulled some blue thread through the weave of her canvas.

"*Are* you too nervous?" Jasmyn asked.

Amber shrugged. "I love singing. But . . . in front of people?"

Jasmyn pushed her glasses up the bridge of her nose. "Maybe if you didn't think of it so much as you singing as much as praising God using the gift He has given you, you would feel less nervous."

Amber stopped stitching. "You mean . . . if I did if for God instead of for me it would be easier?"

"Exactly!" Jasmyn smiled. "Like, since He gave you the gift of a singing voice, anyway. It's a way to say 'thanks' to Him." Then she explained, "My dad is a writer. He writes devotionals and books about prayer. He always says since God gave him the gift of words, he uses them to give God glory."

Amber pressed her lips together. She looked like she was really thinking about what Jasmyn had said.

Jasmyn looked back at the phone and asked suddenly, "Oh, what happened here?"

I looked over at the screen and realized she was at the part when I had put down my phone and began to dance. I laughed and explained.

This time Amber took out her phone. She found the video of my dancing and played it for her. "See?"

"That's a nice dance," Jasmyn said. "Is that from Mallory's music video or something?"

"No," I felt my face grow a little warm. "It's just something I made up."

"So, you're a dancer. Are *you* going to be in the talent show?"

"Not doing this dance," I said. "But I will be in the show!" I then told her all about the Rani situation and even about the difficulties with Mariska and Quinn. "So, I don't know how it's all going to turn out."

"I'm sure you'll do great," Jasmyn said. "I'll come and watch!"

When church was over, Dad invited Jasmyn and her parents to our house. But Jasmyn's parents said they were still getting things settled in their new home and that another day would be better. I was sad that Jasmyn couldn't come over, but glad that she at least *would* be coming over soon.

"And before she comes," I told my family as we were buckling our seatbelts in the car, "we have to make sure there is space for her wheelchair to move around."

"Good idea, Cammie," Dad said approvingly. "I like the way you're anticipating her needs. That's a good way to love your neighbor."

"The dogs might give us the biggest problem," Lena said. She tested to make sure her seatbelt was secure. "They might run in her path or jump on her."

I made a face. "I hope dogs don't scare her!"

"We'll find out and work it out before she comes," Dad assured us.

On Monday morning Amber and I met Jasmyn at her van in front of the school. As we walked her toward the building, Rani and June met us. I introduced them.

"I hope we get to be friends," Rani told Jasmyn, "but I might have to move away soon."

"No, you won't," I insisted.

Jasmyn looked from me to Rani. "I heard about your problem," she said. "Moving is hard, I know."

"Yup," I said. I knew too!

"But," Jasmyn continued, "my father has family in London. And I've been there too. To be honest, I loved it there. It's a fantastic city."

"Really?" Rani brightened.

"Oh, yes!" Jasmyn said. And with June and Amber following the two of them, Jasmyn told Rani more about how great she thought London was.

As I watched them head toward the front doors of the school, I felt my heart begin to race again. It made me nervous to hear Rani sounding so interested in England. Sounding so happy about moving. *Happy,* I thought, my shoulders sagging, *about leaving me.*

"Hey!" I yelled. "Wait for me!" And I sprinted to catch up with them.

Chapter 7

Ms. Roderick and the rest of the class welcomed Jasmyn as soon as she entered the classroom. We showed her to her desk and she looked really happy to find all the rocks decorating the top of it. She admired them all, picked them up one by one, asked who had painted it, and thanked each person. Once class began, Jasmyn had to put all of the painted rocks in a compartment of her powerchair to take home so that she could clear her desk for writing. But she left out one rock. The one I had painted. She had it on top of her desk all morning as she worked. It made me feel really good!

At lunchtime I brought Jasmyn to my table. Mariska and Quinn, who were in the other fifth grade class, and usually sat at a different table, came over with their lunch trays and joined us.

After meeting Jasmyn, they settled in. "So," Mariska said, ignoring her chicken nuggets and going straight for her fruit cup. "We're rehearsing after school again, today, right?"

"Right," I said.

"At my place again," Rani added. "And I have something for all of you."

"You do?" I asked, blinking quickly. "What is it?"

"It's a surprise. You'll see."

Jasmyn flipped her blond hair to look over her shoulder. "What's over there?" she asked Amber.

My sister jumped a little in her seat. "Huh?"

"It's just that you keep looking over to the corner over there." Jasmyn turned her chair a little to look. "Is that the sign-up table for the talent show?" She gasped and turned back to Amber with an excited whisper. "Are you going to enter?"

"Maybe," Amber said, glancing over at the table again.

"Do it now," I nudged her. "Before you change your mind." Then I raised my voice so that the others could hear me, "I'm just going over to the sign-up table to add your names to The Ruby Slippers, okay?"

"Okay. Thanks." Mariska and June replied.

"Come on," I waved my sister over.

When Ms. Greene saw Amber, she pumped her fist in the air. "So, you've decided to let your light shine! Fabulous!" She wrote down Amber's name on the list of acts. "And what song will you be singing, Ms. Daniels?"

"'God is Good' by Mallory Winston," Amber said shyly.

"Great song choice!" Ms. Greene said.

But I felt a pang of jealousy when I heard the song Amber had chosen. I shouldn't have been surprised that she had chosen it. It was what she had been singing with Lena all week, after all. And all the Daniels sisters loved the song. It wasn't even like she was dancing to it. It just made me a little sad that she was getting to sing it at the talent show and I was dancing to something completely different—and a song that wasn't even my choice. *Oh, well,* I sighed to myself. Then, leaning over the table, I told Ms. Greene. "And I just need to add a couple of names to The Ruby Slippers . . ."

When we got back to the table, we didn't tell the others that Amber had signed up because she wanted to keep it quiet. But we gave a secret thumbs-ups to Jasmyn to let her know.

"What about you?" I asked her. "Did you want to sign up for the talent show?"

"Oh, no," Jasmyn said. "I don't sing. And I *used* to dance—before I needed my wheels. But most of the things I do now—like knit or ride horses—you can't exactly do on a stage."

"You ride horses? Really?" I was amazed. We Daniels sisters loved horses.

"Yeah, there's a ranch I go to that offers horseback riding classes for people who need wheelchairs. I ride a beautiful pinto named Sally. I love her."

"Wow. But yeah, you can't exactly bring Sally to the stage, can you?" I said with a giggle. "You know, I never really thought about it before, but there must be a lot of talents people have that can't really be shown on stage."

"Yeah," Amber agreed. She got a faraway look in her eyes. "But if you could bring Sally on stage everybody would love it."

"Everybody," Jasmyn agreed, "except Sally!"

After school I went home with Rani. Her mother drove us and June, Mariska, Quinn to her house to practice. She gave us snacks of crackers and cheese and lemonade. Then Mrs. Harrison led us all to the den where we had practiced before. "Look on the couch, ladies," she said.

Four sets of red dancing slippers were placed on the sofa. Index cards with our names written on them were placed next to each set. We all rushed over in excitement, tried them on, and spoke at once.

"Thank you!"

"How did you do this?"

"How did you know my size?"

"Oh, these fit perfectly!"

In between smiles, nods, and laughs, Ms. Harrison said, "You're welcome!" and "I work for a shoe company, remember? Employee discount!" and "I asked your parents for all your sizes, of course!"

I tried a few moves in my new shoes. I loved the way they looked when I danced. I squealed, "These are great! Thank you so much!"

"You're welcome, sweetie." She gave us all a wave. "Now, I'll let you girls get to work!" Mrs. Harrison said and left the room.

"Okay!" I said immediately. "I found a video of the dance we did at the recital and I've been practicing it all weekend, so I know what we need to do." I pointed at Rani. "Get the music ready." Then I gestured at the couch. "The rest of you help me push this furniture back a little. We need more room."

Everyone followed my instructions except Mariska. She just stood staring at us with her mouth hanging open.

Not wanting her to take over like she did last time, I kept talking. "That side of the couch will be stage left, and this side of the couch will be stage right. Where the coffee table is will be where the audience is. Come on, help me push that back too."

Once I felt there was enough room, I led the girls to the entryway of the den. "Now, Rani: music please. And everyone, follow my lead."

Mariska didn't look too happy about it, but she joined the end of the line as we made our "entrance" onto the "stage."

Our practice was going great for the first twenty minutes or so. That is, until I tried putting Rani in the middle. Since the whole reason we had entered the talent show in the first place was for Rani's sake, I wanted her to be the star. But she kept laughing and shaking her head because the middle person had some extra moves to do and she didn't feel like she was good enough to do them.

Then Mariska pushed her aside. "Like this," she told Rani. She began doing the steps perfectly.

Of course, I thought, and remembered. Not only was Mariska probably the best dancer in the class, but she knew the choreography well because she had danced the middle part at the Christmas recital. (Only there had been five girls doing the middle part then because we had a bigger group.)

Rani watched intently. "I don't think I will be able to remember all that in time for the talent show," she said with a nervous laugh.

"Don't you have a video of the dance? You can practice to it, like I did," I said. "Or I can email you a copy of mine."

Rani chewed on her thumbnail. She still looked unsure.

"Oh, don't force her," Mariska said. "Don't worry, Rani. I'll do it."

I took in a deep breath. "No," I told Mariska. "This is Rani's part. She'll get it. You'll see."

Mariska crossed her arms. "But she just told you she can't."

"But she can," I argued.

"Oh, really? Go ahead, Rani. Show Ashton how you can't." Mariska stomped over to the couch, threw herself into it, and pouted.

"I-I . . ." Rani's eyes got wet and shiny.

I felt my chest grow hot and whirled around to Mariska. "Now look what you did? How can you be so mean?"

"*I'm* mean?" Mariska leapt off the couch. "You're the one trying to force Rani to do something she's not ready to do!"

"I'm not doing anything like that!" I huffed. "I'm saying you have to have patience and let her do it! Not be impatient and take over!"

"Take over?" Mariska shouted. "You're the one who's been bossing the rest of us around since this practice began!"

"*Of course,* I am!" I shouted back. "I *am* the boss! Of this dance troupe, anyway!"

"But you're not even the best dancer!" Mariska said smugly. "I am. I should be the boss."

"You and Quinn joined *my* dance troupe, remember?" I pointed out. "It was my idea in the first place. Even the *name* was my idea. So . . ." and then I surprised myself with what I said next, ". . . if you don't like it, you can leave!"

This time it was Mariska's eyes that got wet and shiny. I felt bad immediately.

"Oh, I'm sor—" I began, but Mariska was red in the face and she yelled over my words.

"If that's what you want, maybe we will quit! Yes, that's it," she grabbed her knapsack and shoes from off the floor. "Quinn and I will both quit. We'll make our own dance troupe and dance in the talent show and we'll be better than you!"

I wanted to say, "No, don't do that!" But I was too angry. Instead I threw my arms out in disgust. "Fine! Do that, then!"

The next thing we knew, Mariska, Rani, and I were all crying.

"Girls, girls, girls!" Mrs. Harrison said, coming into the room. Her face was full of concern and confusion. "What is going on?"

Rani ran into her mother's arms as Mariska and I both pointed to each other and started trying to explain.

"Well, *she* was trying to force Rani to—" Mariska started.

"Actually, *she* was trying to steal Rani's part—" I began.

June covered her ears and sat on a corner of the couch. Quinn stood silently by the door. She was holding her knapsack over her shoulder with one hand and her shoes in the other, waiting for Mariska to tell her what to do.

"Shhh," Mrs. Harrison said. "Rani, why don't you tell me what happened?"

Rani shook her head and shrugged.

"I don't think I want to be in this dance troupe anymore, Mrs. Harrison," Mariska said in a grown-up way. "Quinn and I want to go home. Right, Quinn?"

Quinn nodded but remained silent.

"Can't you girls work this out?" Mrs. Harrison asked, wrinkling her forehead with concern.

I looked down at my "ruby slippers" for a moment, wishing I really *could* click my heels together and magically be whisked home. Finally, I said, "Yes." Whenever my sisters and I had arguments, Dad and Aunt Sam made us talk things out and try to come to a solution. Or at least apologize to each other. So, I apologized first. "I'm sorry, Mariska."

"I'm sorry too," Mariska said back. But she mumbled it, so it sounded like "Mmsrytoo." She sadly traced a semicircle on the floor with the toe of one of her new slippers. Then she perked up and looked me in the eye. "So, can I dance the middle part?"

I couldn't believe she asked that, but I didn't look away. Instead, I took a deep breath and spoke in even tones. "No . . . Like I said before: that part is for Rani."

"But like *I* said before, Rani doesn't want it. Do you, Rani?" Mariska looked sidelong at her.

But Rani didn't seem to know what to say. She knew she'd be upsetting one of her two friends no matter which answer she gave.

At that moment a car horn honked.

"Oh, just forget it!" Mariska said. "That's my Mom. We're going, Quinn, come on." She nodded at Mrs. Harrison. "Thank you for the snack and the shoes." And with that, the two girls left. Mrs. Harrison followed them to make sure they got out okay, leaving me, Rani, and June to just stare at each other in awkward silence.

"I don't want them to quit!" Rani said, finally, with a quaver in her voice.

I took my red dancing slippers off. "It's my fault." I grabbed my sneakers. "I shouldn't have told them to leave."

June frowned. "Maybe." She put an arm around Rani's shoulders. "But you should be the one dancing in the middle, Rani."

Mrs. Harrison came back to the room. "Ashton, your Dad's outside now too."

"Okay, thanks, Mrs. Harrison," I said.

She watched me tie my sneakers. "Is there anything I can do to help?" she asked. "I told Mariska's mother that I was sure you girls would be able to work things out amongst yourselves. But if there is any way I can help you girls, please, let me know."

"Don't worry, Mrs. Harrison," I said, wanting to comfort not just her, but Rani and June too. "It'll all be fine by tomorrow. I'm sure of it."

But as I left the house and headed toward the car, I had to admit to myself that I wasn't sure at all.

Chapter 8

Uh-oh," Dad said, taking a look at my face as I slid into the car. "Problems at rehearsal again?"

"Mariska wants to be in charge *and* be the star of the show," I blurted. "Now she's quit and taken Quinn with her, and Rani's all upset." I groaned. "In other words, yes, problems at rehearsal again."

Dad nodded to show he was listening while he kept his eyes on the road. "So, what's going to happen now? Will you girls continue without the others? Or . . . ?"

"You're not going to ask me if I'm going to quit, too, are you? I don't quit, Dad. At least not that easily." I played with my bracelet, sliding it up and down my forearm. "No, we're going to go on, but I'm not only going to have to figure out a way to get Mariska and Quinn to come back to The Ruby Slippers, but also to get them to do things my way when they *do* come back." I groaned again.

"Can I ask you something?" Dad pulled to a stop at a light. "Is it important that everything goes exactly *your* way with this dance? I mean, can you compromise a little with Mariska? Would that help things?"

"Compromise? What do you mean?"

"I mean, you give in a little and she gives in a little. You find a way to each get something you want and cooperate with one another."

"I don't know, Dad. I'm just asking her to follow the choreography and to not steal the spotlight." I scratched my forehead. "Am I supposed to let her do whatever she wants just to keep the peace?"

My father shrugged. "Maybe you don't need her in the dance?"

"We could do it without her . . . and Quinn. Only Rani wants them in the dance now. And she's all upset that they quit. And . . . I guess I just don't like Rani being upset."

Since she was my friend, seeing Rani upset made *me* upset. I was also worried because Mrs. Harrison had seen The Ruby Slippers practice twice already and both times it had not ended well. How were we girls supposed to convince her that Rani needed to stay with her friends—and be in this show—if all Mrs. Harrison saw at our rehearsals were arguments and tears?

As Dad pulled up to the house, I admitted to him, "I don't know what I'm going to do."

"Well, then," Dad said, reaching out and giving me a quick stroke on the cheek. "You know what I'm going to say, don't you?"

I shook my head.

"Give it to God," Dad said. "When a problem becomes too heavy for you, just give it to God. Stop trying to figure it out yourself and put it in his hands."

"I understand that we can show God love when we show kindness and love to other people," I said. "It's in Matthew 25. But giving Him your problems sounds almost . . . I don't know. A little mean. Problems don't sound like very nice presents to give to God."

"But actually, they are, sweetie. God loves us very much.

And when you give Him your problems to take care of, it shows that you have real faith in Him. It makes him very happy!"

"Really?" I raised an eyebrow.

"Really. It shows that you know that no problem is too big or difficult for God to overcome because He is an awesome God. He wants us to trust Him. It's even in Scripture. Like in 1 Peter 5:7: 'Cast all your anxiety on him because he cares for you.'"

It would be a relief not to worry about the talent show, I thought to myself.

"Would you like to say a prayer?" Dad asked.

I nodded.

"Come on, let's go to the porch then."

Dad and I walked up to the house, but instead of going inside, we sat together on the porch swing. We began to gently swing as he placed my hands in his, closed his eyes, and said, "Dear Lord, it is written 'Do not be anxious about anything, but in every situation, by prayer and petition, with thanksgiving, present your requests to God. And the peace of God, which transcends all understanding, will guard your hearts and your minds in Christ Jesus.' So, I present to you my daughter, Ashton, who is going to make her request known to you." He opened his eyes and nodded encouragingly at me.

I closed my eyes, then, too, and said, "God, you know the problems I'm having with this whole talent show thing. I don't know how to solve them, so . . ." I opened my eyes. Dad was still nodding, urging me to continue, so I closed my eyes again. ". . . I'm giving the whole problem with Mariska and Quinn over to you. Thank you. Amen."

"Amen!" Dad echoed with a smile of satisfaction.

"Dad?" I asked as he unlocked the front door.

"Yes?"

"How will I know when God has answered my prayer?"

"You'll know." Dad sounded very sure about it.

After that, I went upstairs to my bedroom to do as much of my homework as I could before dinner. As I worked on my math problems, my *life* problems kept trying to creep back into my mind. But I kept pushing those thoughts away. *I'm not going to try to solve those problems,* I told myself. *That's God's homework. I'll let him do that, while I do mine.*

When I was finished, I closed my notebook and pushed my stack of books off to the side. When I did this, they knocked one of the painted rocks off the desk. I stretched out my hand just in time to catch it before it hit the ground.

I opened my palm and read its message. *God is Good.*

Just then I became aware of humming coming from the top bunk bed. It was coming from Amber, who was working on her homework too. She was sitting up there, dangling one of her legs off the side, and of course, humming "God is Good."

I got up from my seat and waved at her. "Start from the beginning," I said. And she did—only singing this time. And I began to do my dream-dance again, sometimes even dancing around my desk chair and using it as a prop. It was the first time I had been able to physically perform the whole dance that was in my head, and it felt wonderful. It made me feel sort of like the butterfly I had painted on the rock: happy, light, and free. Especially when I danced during the chorus.

I will sing praises to the Lord
For God is good.
God is good

In the dark and in the light.
God is good.
I'll sing praises to the Lord
Throughout the day,
Throughout the night.
Because through everything and all
God is good.

When the song was over and I was in my final pose with my head bowed, all these memories flooded my mind at once: like Rani's bad news and why we had even signed up for the talent show in the first place.

"That's it!" I shouted. I straightened and looked up at a startled Amber. "I know what to do about Mariska and Quinn."

"O . . . kay . . ." Amber said. "Um, what?"

I raised a finger in the air. "I'm going to tell them the truth!"

Chapter 9

Did you lie to them before or something?" Amber still didn't know what I meant.

"No, no," I explained. "But I didn't tell them the truth. That is, not the whole truth." I began to pace up and down the rug in front of the bunk beds. "But that's it! Once I do, they'll come back. I just know it!" I looked up at the ceiling. "Thank you, God!"

"Amber! Ashton!" Aunt Sam's voice called up to us. "Dinner's ready!"

Suddenly, I was super-hungry. "Beat you there!" I told Amber mischievously since I was closest to the door.

Amber's mouth fell open. "No fair!"

And we both laughed the whole way downstairs.

"You two sound happy," Dad said as Amber and I took our places at the table. "Was that you I heard singing up there, Amber?"

Amber nodded. "Mm-hm."

"Yeah," I added. "She was practicing." Then I covered my mouth. "Oops," I said under my breath. I didn't want to give away her news.

It was too late. "What happened? What's the big secret?" Dad asked as Ansley and Lena joined us at the kitchen table. They looked as us questioningly.

Amber grinned. "I'm going to sing in the talent show."

Congratulations rang out as everyone let Amber know how proud of her they all were.

"With the two of you in the show," Ansley said, "one of us will have to be the cameraman for a change."

"I'll film every second of your performance," Dad promised. "Both of your performances, that is."

"Thanks, Dad." I watched as Aunt Sam served me some chicken. "Just make sure when you record my dance that you get all *five* of us." I said that to let him know that I expected to make up with Mariska and Quinn and for all of us to be able to dance together at the show.

"Understood," Dad said. "That's my girl." He winked at me and then turned to Ansley. "And what about you, Ans? How was your math test today?"

"Well . . ." Ansley said. "At least it's over. So, I don't have to freak out over taking it anymore. Now I can just freak out over what my grade will be."

We laughed with understanding. We all knew what those feelings were like!

"One thing is for sure," Dad said. "And that's that you did your best. So, no matter what your grade is, if you know you put in your best effort, you can be proud of yourself. When will you get your test back? Tomorrow?"

Ansley shuddered. "Tomorrow might be too soon!"

Not for me, I thought, as I bowed my head for prayer. With what I knew I needed to settle with Mariska and Quinn, tomorrow couldn't come soon enough.

The next morning, I was the first one up. I brushed my teeth, and put on my uniform, and was at the breakfast table before anyone else. I don't know where I got the idea that if I did everything faster and earlier than usual it would somehow make all my sisters faster and earlier than usual too. Because that's not what happened at all!

First Lena couldn't find a clean uniform to wear. (Aunt Sam had done the laundry, but Lena had forgotten to put it away.)

Next Ansley got up late because she was having a nice dream that she didn't want to end. (She mumbled something about "unicorns" at the breakfast table.)

Then Amber almost tripped over Zette and ended up spilling her breakfast cereal all over the floor.

And finally, just when we were ready to go, Aunt Sam couldn't find her car keys. Dad had left early in the other car, so we all spread out around the house looking for them. It was unusual for her to misplace them. She usually left them in a bowl by the door. But yesterday someone had called her just when she was entering the house, and she ended up bringing them into the kitchen with the groceries as she spoke on the phone. Lena found the keys inside of the pantry behind some pancake mix!

All these delays caused us to almost be late for school. The front lawns were empty when the Daniels sisters all ran into the three separate school buildings. Amber and I got into our classroom a second before the late bell rang.

I was not as upset about being late as I was about not being able to see Mariska and Quinn before school began. I just wanted to fix things between us as soon as possible.

"But now I'll have to wait for lunchtime . . ." I grumbled to myself. I threw myself down into my chair and sagged.

"Are you okay?" Jasmyn asked.

"Yes, and . . . no," I whispered as Ms. Roderick took attendance. This time she was wearing earrings that looked like tongues of flame. "It's kind of a long story, but basically our talent show rehearsal didn't go so great." I kept my eyes on Ms. Roderick. I didn't want to get in trouble for talking. Especially since I got there just before the late bell. "I'll tell you about it at lunch."

Ms. Roderick looked at me just then. "Were you talking about me?" she asked brightly.

"What?" I asked, startled. "No . . ."

"Oh, because my ears were burning," she said. And she pointed to her earrings with the pencil she held in her hand.

I groaned but laughed too.

At lunchtime, Amber and I walked with Jasmyn, and I told her all about my rehearsal problems and my talk with Dad. ". . . and after praying about it and giving it to God, I was able to put it out of my mind for a while. And then I understood something," I said. I started talking faster as I grew more excited. "We never told Mariska and Quinn about how Rani might move away and how we don't want her to. We never told them that trying to keep her here was the reason we had even signed up for the talent show in the first place."

Jasmyn raised her eyebrows. "You didn't tell them? But you told me."

"Yeah! I know! Weird, huh? I guess I didn't tell them at first because it was sort of a private thing between us friends, you know? Me, Rani, and June. And Amber, of course. It was our secret plan. And then, when we ended up having rehearsals at Rani's place and I didn't want to talk about it and have

Mrs. Harrison overhear us or anything, because again, secret plan."

"That wouldn't have ruined everything," Amber said.

"But now, now I'm going to tell them," I concluded.

"Because you think that once they hear your story, they'll *want* to help?" Jasmyn asked after thinking about everything I had just told her.

"Exactly."

"I hope it works, then," Jasmyn said encouragingly.

"It's got to. I don't think it was my idea! I believe God gave it to me," I confessed. I waved at Rani and June who were sitting in their usual places. "Well, I see those two," I said. I took a sweeping glance around the cafeteria. "But where are . . ." Then I saw Mariska and Quinn. They were standing by the talent show sign-up table! I gasped. "Amber, you stay with Jasmyn. I've got to stop them!"

I charged over to the sign-up table. They looked up just as I arrived, "I'm glad I caught you," I said.

Mariska and Quinn exchanged glances. "You're too late," Mariska said, crossing her arms. "We've already signed up as our own dance troupe," she paused. "The Red Shoes."

It was my turn to cross my arms. "You're kidding. The Red Shoes? Really?"

"It's a famous ballet story," Quinn said stubbornly, stepping forward.

I made a face. Ballet would never be my favorite form of dance. No matter how pretty it looked, I just didn't like dancing it the same way I did modern or hip-hop.

"Besides," Mariska said throwing her hands up. "We still have those red shoes to dance in."

That's true, I admitted to myself. Anyway, *I hadn't come to argue. I'd come to make up.* "That's great," I said, trying to sound enthusiastic. "Maybe you'd like to be in two dance troupes in the talent show instead of just one?" The grin I offered her was tight with anticipation.

Mariska narrowed her eyes. "What do you mean?" she asked. "You still want us in The Ruby Slippers?"

"Yes," I said, swallowing hard. "And so does June, and so does Rani. Rani especially. But I need to tell you two something about Rani that I didn't tell you before . . ." And I finally told them the whole truth about her maybe having to move. "So, you see," I ended, "she has to be the star. That's why I wanted her to be in the middle. I want her parents to see that she's needed here. That she's special to us."

Mariska and Quinn were silent for a moment. But I could tell they were both thinking about the new information that I had just given them.

"But what happens if she ends up moving after all?" Quinn said finally.

"Well, if she does, you can be the one to dance in the middle," I said, trying not to wince. It hadn't been an easy thing to say, but it had felt like the right thing to say. It was like what Dad had said about compromising. If she gave in a little, I had to give in a little.

"Hmm," Mariska looked off into the distance.

I clucked my tongue. "Well? Are you two going to help or not?"

Quinn looked at Mariska, as usual, waiting for her to give her answer.

"Yes," Mariska said. "I'll help. We both will. In fact, I'll even teach Rani the steps for the middle part if she wants me to."

"That's so nice of you!" I said, clasping my hands together. "I know that will make her feel a lot better. Thanks, you guys. Let's go tell her!"

Chapter 10

The expression on Rani's face when she saw all three of us smiling and heading toward the table together made me giggle. Her dark eyes looked bigger and darker than ever, and her dark eyebrows were raised so high they reached the top of her forehead.

"What's going on?" she asked. I could hear the hope in her voice.

"What's going on is that we're all going to dance together," I said.

"And we're going to do a great job!" Mariska added. "And if you need any help with practicing the middle part, I can show you what you need to do."

"Why?" Rani asked in a small voice. "How?"

Quinn pumped a fist in the air. "It's Operation Keep Rani Home!"

"Actually, it's Operation There's No Place Like Home!" I said.

Then everyone at the table, chanted at the same time, "There's no place like home! There's no place like home! There's no place like home!"

We had a little meeting right then and there and decided we'd ask our parents if we could have another rehearsal—even if was just for half an hour—after dance class, since we'd all be at Tambourine Studios together. As we chattered on, I caught a glimpse of Jasmyn looking down at her meal, not saying a word. *I think she might be . . . sad,* I thought to myself. Then I realized that she was the only girl at the table who wasn't going to be in the talent show. *Maybe she feels left out.* The thought made my heart hurt for her. I wasn't sure what I could say or do to help her, so I decided to change the subject. I pointed to the throw blanket she had on over her legs.

"That's pretty," I said. "I noticed it this morning. Did you knit that?"

"Yes," Jasmyn said, lighting up as all the others turned to look and oooh and ahhh. "But actually, it's crocheted, not knitted. Knitting takes two needles. Crocheting takes one needle—it's a hook, really."

It was a cozy lap-warmer, made up of square patterns, in blues and greens that matched the school uniform.

"Pretty," Amber said. "It looks like it's made up of tiles."

"Those are called granny squares," Jasmyn said. "I can show you how to make them."

"I'd love to learn!" Amber's eyes sparkled at the idea.

"Okay," Jasmyn said, excitedly noticing Amber's sincere interest, "maybe I'll show you a few things when I come over!"

"How many crochet hooks do you have?" I asked, smiling-yet-serious. "I have the feeling that all the Daniels sisters are going to want to give it a try. And . . . do you have any pink yarn?"

"Oh, I have plenty of hooks—and yarn too. Pink, blue, green, yellow, purple—and of course, orange."

"It can be, like, a crocheting party!" Amber said.

Rani pouted. "That sounds like fun! Can I come?"

"Me too!" June piped up.

Jasmyn hesitated, unsure of what to say.

"Hey, yeah!" I said, giving it some thought. "Maybe it should actually be a party. This Sunday after church!"

"At our place," Amber caught on, "to welcome you to the neighborhood!"

Mariska and Quinn, who I'd never had over to my place, wanted to come too. So Amber and I spent the rest of lunch period working out the details.

"What if you're Dad says 'no'?" Quinn asked after we'd pretty much planned out the whole thing.

"Oh, we have people over to the house on Sunday afternoons all the time." I explained. "It's sort of a tradition with us. He won't say 'no.'" I assured her. "You'll see."

Later that day, when we were back home, Amber, Ansley, Lena, and I gathered around the kitchen counter to have our after-school snack.

"What do you think?" I asked Aunt Sam, as I opened a packet of string cheese. "Isn't it a great idea?"

"I like it," Aunt Sam agreed. "But we'll have to ask your dad first. He might have plans."

We decided to FaceTime him right then and there. Amber and I huddled around Aunt Sam's phone. When Dad's smiling face popped up on the screen, we both started talking at the same time.

Dad went from concerned (at first, he seemed to think it was an emergency) to laughing. "One at a time! One at a time!"

Finally, Amber and I took turns explaining the party idea, managing to make some kind of sense.

"Sounds like you managed to make up with Mariska and Quinn," Dad said to me. The approval in his voice rang out loud and clear. He was happy for me.

"Yup!" I said, swiveling a little in the stool I was sitting in. "So, can we?"

"I don't see why not. It's a good way to continue to be friends with Mariska and Quinn and to welcome Jasmyn and her family into the neighborhood."

"We're welcoming the stranger!" I crowed. "Though Jasmyn isn't really much of a stranger anymore," I admitted.

"You're still doing a good thing," Dad said. "Because you're loving your neighbor. Or make that neighbors." Then he addressed Aunt Sam, "Well, sis, I guess that means you've got some shopping to do."

Aunt Sam flashed him a thumbs-up. "I'm on it," she told him.

During the conversation, Ansley had been sort of skipping around the kitchen, stopping to take out a mixing bowl from one cabinet and stooping to take out a baking tray from another.

"What's all that banging around?" Dad asked.

I turned the phone around so that he could see Ansley tying on her unicorn apron.

"It's Ansley. It looks like she's getting ready to bake something."

Ansley lifted a shaker filled with cinnamon and waved it at Daddy. "I promised myself that if I scored a ninety or higher on my math test I'd make cinnamon rolls for everyone," she said.

Cinnamon rolls were Ansley's specialty and a favorite of everyone in the house. And Dad, especially, loved anything cinnamon.

We all gasped. "Does that mean you passed?" Lena asked.

"I got a hundred!"

We all cheered and clapped. Even Dad on the small screen of the phone.

"That's great Ansley!" Aunt Sam said. "But shouldn't I be baking you something as a reward? This way it's kind of like you're baking a reward for everyone else."

Ansley looked at her in surprise. "Are you kidding? Baking *is* my reward! I love baking so much!"

"You should make these every time you pass a test," I suggested with a giggle.

"I don't know about that," Ansley said, giggling too, as she poured flour into the bowl. "But maybe I could whip up a fresh batch of these on Sunday, too, for when your friends come over."

"That'd be great!" My mouth watered at the thought of having fresh cinnamon rolls twice in one week. "It's the perfect 'Ansley' way to welcome the stranger—or love your neighbor. Or both!"

Ansley, who had started mixing her ingredients, stopped suddenly and looked me in the eye. "You've given me a great idea!"

"I have?" My last piece of string cheese dangled from my mouth as I stared at her in surprise.

"Yes, you have! But I want it to be a surprise. So . . . shoo!" She waved us all away. "Get out of the kitchen, all of you!" she said.

Whatever the surprise was, I was sure it was going to be a yummy one. So I had no problem obeying Ansley and ran up the stairs to change out of my uniform.

Once I was in a comfy pair of shorts and a T-shirt, I began dancing around the room. I was in such a good mood. Everything was working out so well. Mariska and Quinn were back in the talent show with us, Ansley had done well on her test, and we were even going to have a party that weekend.

"God is good, God is good," I sang in a low voice to myself.

And I began dancing my special dance to the Mallory Winston song just as Amber came into the room.

"Is that the dance you'll be doing at the talent show?" she asked. She sat on my bed and watched.

"No, that one's different. This is the dance that I made up," I explained.

"Oh." Amber pulled herself further into the bed. "Why don't you perform this at the talent show too?"

I froze. "What?"

"I said why don't you perform your dance at the talent show too? Couldn't you?"

"I-I don't know." I tried to imagine dancing a solo after dancing with The Ruby Slippers. "I don't think there'd be time for two dances."

"I mean can't you sign up to do a different act? A solo act, like me?" Amber asked. "Didn't you tell me that Mariska and Quinn will also be dancing their own dance as The Red Shoes? So, they'll be performing two dances, won't they? Or have they decided they don't want to anymore?"

I had forgotten about The Red Shoes. "Hmmm." I said. "Good question. Or should I say good questions?" And as I thought about what Amber said, I began to feel like I was a balloon getting slowly pumped up with helium. *What if I did sign up? What if I was able to get a spot of my own in the talent show? What if I got to perform my dance and make my daydream come true?* I danced around the outline of the small rug in front of my bed. *It would be so cool! But . . . will I really be able to memorize and perform two dances in just a few short weeks?* I wondered. I glanced up at Amber. *Was she still waiting for me to answer her?*

Finally, I shrugged, and said out loud, "I'll think about it."

But inside my heart I had already decided: *I'll do it!* I wasn't sure how I would be able to without the others seeing me, but . . . *I'll sign up tomorrow!* I told myself. And, feeling joyful, I twirled around the room again and again.

Chapter 11

"Ta-da!" Ansley shouted.

Dinner was over and it was now time to have some of the fresh incredible-smelling cinnamon rolls.

Ansley laid the tray down on the center of the table. "Surprise!"

The cinnamon rolls were all shaped like hearts!

Everyone at the table had something to say.

"Those look incredible!"

"So cute!"

"Amazing, Ansley!"

I curled my hands and brought them together at the center of my chest. "I heart it!"

"How'd you make them?" Amber asked.

"It was easy. Well, I looked it up online, first. But what you do is instead of rolling the strips in a swirl, you pinch the strips in the middle. Then you curl the two equal sides up and inward toward one another. Then you lay them on the tray like this, upside down and right-side up, side by side. Some come out better than others," she admitted.

"I think they all look great," Dad said.

"And they all taste awesome," I said licking some icing off the tip of one of my fingers.

"Thanks! I think I'll make them like this for the party too," Ansley said. "Because it shows love of neighbor! Get it?"

"Oh, I get it!" I said, lifting a plate and handing it to her. "And I'd like to get some now, please. I pointed to a fat one in the middle. "Dibs!"

That night, as Amber climbed up the ladder to her bunk, I got down on my knees and prayed at my bedside.

"Thank you, God," I whispered. "You really are good. You helped me so much with the talent show. Thank you for showing me how to make peace with Mariska and Quinn. Thank you for helping me make Rani happy. Thank you, too, for the party idea to welcome Jasmyn. Thank you for all the ways you are showing me to love my neighbor, because when we love our neighbor, I know we're really loving you!" I opened my eyes and was about to crawl into my cozy bed when I had one final thought, "Oh! And please let our rehearsal tomorrow go well! Thank you, again. In Jesus' name, Amen."

But it wasn't rehearsal that was running through my mind when I woke up the next morning. Instead, all I could think about was signing up for the talent show on my own. So, like the day before, I got up and was ready before everyone else. This time, at least, there were no disasters, though, and we all managed to go to school at the regular time.

When we got there and Aunt Sam saw Jasmyn's van pulling in, she got out of the car with us to chat with Mr. and Mrs. Wright and discuss the party.

"I'll be bringing lots of yarn and supplies," Jasmyn said when she got out of her van and rolled over to me and Amber. Her face glowed with anticipation. "I was thinking of making a prayer shawl."

"Ooh, that sounds wonderful! I want to make one too," Amber said.

Jasmyn nodded with understanding. "But you should probably start with something smaller. Like a hat or a scarf. Don't worry, I'll show you."

Amber clapped her hands. "It's going to be so fun!"

As we headed for the school buildings, I caught sight of Mariska and Rani in the distance. They were dancing in unison on the front lawn.

Mariska's going over the steps with Rani just like she said she would, I thought gratefully. It warmed my heart to see it.

When we caught up with them (and June and Quinn), Rani's face was glowing with sweat and happiness. "Oh, I think I'm getting it now," she said. "I'm so relieved."

"Great!" I said, "I think we should practice during recess too. What do you guys think?"

Everyone immediately agreed.

"Even though my mom called Tambourine and they said we could stay a half hour longer in the studio after class to practice," Rani said. "The more practice the better."

I exchanged glances with Amber. "Your *mom* did that? That's a good sign."

Rani nodded. "She saw how upset I was last time."

"And she did say she wanted to help us," I remembered. "This is great news!" With Rani's mom on our side, more than half the battle was won. I was feeling very hopeful about what Rani's dad's decision might be. *But that doesn't mean we shouldn't practice,* I reminded myself. *After all, practice makes perfect.*

I could hardly wait until recess so that we could do just that. But when recess came, there was something else I wanted to do even more—sign up for the talent show for my solo performance! So I sat and waited for everyone to finish their lunches inside the cafeteria.

When everyone seemed to be done or on their last bites, I spoke up, "We best get to practicing outside, right, everyone?"

"Yeah!" The other dancers scrambled to their feet and started heading for the doors that led to the yard. "Let's go!"

"I'm right behind you!" I called out to their backs. Then I turned to Amber and Jasmyn who were about to follow them. "What are you guys going to do?"

"While you rehearse, we'll have our own fun," Amber said. "Right, Jasmyn?"

Jasmyn smiled. "Yeah." She pointed with her thumb at the bag that was slung across the back of her chair. "I'm going to show Amber how to crochet a little."

"What?" I pouted. "Without me?"

Jasmyn's forehead wrinkled in worry. "It's just that I think it'll be easier for me to teach you all one at a time instead of all at the same time. It's close-up work. You know, with small details. You'll be able to see it better when it's one-on-one."

"I guess," I said. I curled my hands into fists and clutched them at my sides. "But I still don't think it's fair." I stomped my foot. But when I saw that Jasmyn's forehead was still wrinkled, I tried to turn my pout into a smile to show her that I wasn't really angry at *her.* I was more annoyed with Amber's head start. I felt like I was really going to be missing out.

If only I could be with Amber at her crocheting lesson today instead of practicing the dance, I grumbled to myself. Then I had an idea. "Kitty," I said to Amber, "Why don't you *film* your lesson? That way I can watch it later and learn from the same lesson as you?"

She made a face. "But I want to be crocheting, not filming."

"But it's not really fair if you get a lesson without me," I said. "Plus you can take close-ups of her fingers to look at it later if you forget how to do any of it. Come on!"

"I don't know."

"I would do it for you," I said.

Amber clucked her tongue.

I put my hands on my hips.

Jasmyn watched us both until Amber finally sagged. "Oh, fine," she said with a groan.

"Great!" I clapped my hands. "Film everything!"

"Yeah, yeah."

I waved cheerfully at them both. "Catch you two later!" And after the two of them finally left, I hurried over to the sign-up table.

When I reached her, Ms. Greene was collecting index cards and pens from the table and throwing them in a cardboard box.

"Oh," I said, hearing the ballpoint pens fall with dull clattering sounds at the bottom of the box. "Are you packing up? I was going to sign up one more act."

"Oh, honey, I'm sorry," Ms. Greene said. "But there's no more room."

My heart slid down to my stomach with a plop. "What?"

"We're all booked up. I even have some names on a waiting list." She pulled a clipboard from out of the cardboard box. "Do you want me to add your name to it?"

I shook my head. "No. Never mind. It was just a thought." I waved. "Forget it."

Rows of wrinkles appeared on her forehead. "Are you sure,

honey? Because the talent show is two and a half weeks away. You never know. A slot could open up."

I pressed my lips together. I really didn't think it was going to happen.

"We want to keep it so that an equal number of kids from each grade get to participate," Ms. Greene went on. "But if someone drops out at the last minute . . ." She twirled a pen between two fingers like a mini baton.

I just knew that wasn't going to happen. Still, I sighed loudly. "Oh, all right." And I added my name to the waiting list.

When I was done, Ms. Greene put the clipboard back in the cardboard box. "That's my girl!" She winked at me. "Good luck!"

"Thanks," I said in a dull voice. Hanging my head, I dragged my feet away from the table. But as I walked further away from it and closer to the exit doors (and the girls practicing outside) I forced myself to walk straighter and straighter. I didn't want any of the others to know that I was upset. Since I hadn't told any of them that I was going to sign up for the talent show on my own, I didn't want any of them finding out that I had tried to do so—and failed. *Especially Mariska and Quinn.*

By the time I reached Mariska and Quinn, not to mention June and Rani, I was all smiles even though I didn't really feel happy in my heart. *I would make a good actress,* I realized. I clapped my hands. "So, what are we do—?" I stopped short. The girls were doing ballet moves! I began to yell. "What *are* you doing? Stop! Stop! Just stop! No ballet! No changes in the choreography! Remember?"

"Oh, relax!" Mariska snapped. "You were taking so long that Quinn and I began practicing our Red Shoes dance instead. Then we began showing Rani and June how it's supposed to go."

Rani nodded as she lifted a leg in a graceful arabesque pose and grinned at me. For some reason seeing her happily copying Mariska's ballet moves made my stomach burn in anger.

"Come on. We don't have a lot of time," I said, stepping into the middle of everyone and stopping their dance. "Let's get back to doing what we're really supposed to be doing. We probably only have ten minutes left for recess."

I was right. We ended up having a very short rehearsal, but that was okay, since after school we would all rehearse again after our dance lesson at Tambourine Studios.

When we got to Tambourine, we quickly changed in the locker room and then, chatting and laughing, we hurried out to the dance floor. But once we entered the studio, we suddenly all fell silent. Ms. Mandy was waiting for all of us there, sitting in a wheelchair!

"Oh, my gosh!"

"What happened?"

"Are you okay?"

We all crowded around our teacher in shock and concern.

Ms. Mandy closed her eyes and held up her hands. "I'm fine, girls, I'm fine. It's just an ankle injury. I'm not supposed to put any pressure on it."

We looked down at her legs, which were both on leg rests. One was bent at the knee in a typical seated position. The other was wrapped in padding and sticking straight out.

"Did you hurt yourself dancing?" I asked.

Ms. Mandy danced with a professional ballet company

when she wasn't teaching classes. "Yes, it was an accident. We were practicing a routine, and as my partner lifted me up, he mis-stepped and wobbled, almost dropping me. I didn't want to fall on my face, so I tried to land on my feet, and I landed wrong."

The students made faces, sucked in their teeth, and made all sorts of sympathetic sounds.

"Ow," I said, thinking about how it must have hurt.

"It's a fracture," Ms. Mandy continued, "and I can get around on crutches. But since I had class with you girls today, I believe it will be easier for me to teach you from this wheelchair."

"Wait a minute . . . you're still going to teach us?" I asked. "How?"

"Watch me," Ms. Mandy said with a smile. Then, turning her chair to face the mirror in front of us, she clapped her hands. "Places, ladies!" she said, and watched our reflections as we all hurried to stand where we usually did.

Then Ms. Mandy lifted her arms in graceful arches. "Let's start with some warm up exercises," she said with a nod at the piano player. "Annnnd ONE! Two, three, four, five, six, seven, eight . . ."

I was amazed with how well Ms. Mandy was able to lead us even though she couldn't use her feet. She danced with her arms, with her facial expressions, and even in the way she turned the chair left, right, and in a circle. And even though she was using a manual wheelchair and not a powerchair, I couldn't help but think of Jasmyn. I was sure she could do the same kinds of turns with her joystick. In fact, the first time I had seen Jasmyn I saw her do a little spin in her wheelchair right after coming out of her van.

Then, I began picturing Jasmyn in place of Ms. Mandy, doing the same kind of graceful moves in time to the music. *I bet Jasmyn can* still *dance if she wants to,* I thought excitedly. *It would be different than the way she used to dance, but it's still dancing. Look at the way Ms. Mandy is telling a story with her gestures and face.* I began to get an idea. An idea that made my heart pound.

Maybe Jasmyn can *dance,* I thought. *Maybe Jasmyn can be a Ruby Slipper!*

Chapter 12

I could hardly wait to tell the others about my idea. But I knew I would have to wait for our class to be over before I could. This got me so distracted that I ended up having a hard time remembering the new choreography again. But when class was finally over and we were about to use the studio for our rehearsal, I sprung it on them.

"Isn't it a great idea?" I asked them all. "Of course, we'd have to figure out where to . . ." I drifted off when I realized no one looked as excited as I felt. "What? You don't think it's a great idea?"

Rani spoke first. "It's not that," she said carefully. "I mean, it's a cool idea, really. It's just that, we don't have a lot of time to rehearse as it is. And to bring in a new dancer . . ."

"Yeah." Mariska crossed her arms. "And it sounds like we would need to change choreography. Aren't you always saying that we aren't allowed to change any of the choreography?"

"Not to mention," June chimed in, "you don't even know if Jasmyn will *want* to dance with us . . ."

"Okay! Okay!" I huffed. "What do you think, Quinn? You haven't said anything."

Quinn shrugged and half-hid behind Mariska. She obviously didn't want to say what she felt, and always just agreed with Mariska anyway.

"I still think it's a cool idea," I grumbled.

"It *is* a cool idea," Rani said, placing a hand on one of my shoulders. "But maybe not for the talent show. Okay?"

I sighed.

"Come on," Mariska pointed at the phone in my hand. "Why don't you put on the music? We don't want to lose any time."

"Fine." I pressed "play" as the other girls all fell in line to make their "entrance."

We had another good rehearsal, but my heart wasn't in it. I couldn't help imagining Jasmyn dancing with us and what that might look like. Plus, I was still stinging from the less-than-enthusiastic reactions the girls had shown my idea. Even though I understood some of the reasons why they said "no," they had all said "no" so fast that it made me worry they were excluding Jasmyn. That they didn't even want to give her a chance because she was in a wheelchair.

And my disappointment showed. I didn't chat. I didn't laugh. I didn't even smile. I just didn't feel like it. And I could tell this made the other girls uneasy, because throughout our practice they kept shooting me worried looks.

Then, about five minutes before rehearsal was over, I had another idea. *Maybe,* I thought again, feeling that same heart-thumping excitement that I felt before, *I can teach Jasmyn the choreography in private. And then maybe she'll be able to join The Ruby Slippers as a surprise! When they see that she can do it, they'll have to change their minds!* These thoughts brought back the smile to my face and the energy to my dancing.

Rani looked relieved to see me more like my regular self.

In fact, we were *all* smiling (and talking) by the time we left the locker room and met Rani's mom in the waiting area. When

Mrs. Harrison came up to us, she examined each of our faces in turn. "Well, don't you all look happy," she said, beaming at us. "Looks like it was a good rehearsal."

"Yes, it was!" Rani grabbed her mother in a quick hug. "And we had a rehearsal at lunchtime that went really well too."

"That's great news!" Mrs. Harrison gave her daughter a few pats on the back. "I'm glad to see you all getting along well."

Rani nodded. "I've made lots of good friends here."

The rest of us all jumped in to agree.

"Yeah!"

"Mm-hmm."

"That's right."

We all wanted Mrs. Harrison to see it would be a bad idea to take Rani away. "Nothing can tear us apart," I said, nudging Rani a little.

Rani nudged me back with a smile.

"Speaking of making friends," Mrs. Harrison said, turning to me, "we got your dad's invitation to Jasmyn's welcome party this Sunday. We'll be there."

"Great!" I said, with a little twirl.

"Yeah, great," Rani said, surprising me with her less-than-enthusiastic voice. Then she tugged on her mother's arm and tried to lead her out the door. "Can we go now?"

Mrs. Harrison nodded, gesturing at me to follow them since she was going to drive me home too. "And I thought it would be nice," she continued, "to give Jasmyn a little present. What do you think if I give her red slippers like the ones I gave you girls? That way she won't feel left out of the group."

Rani immediately made a face. "But that doesn't make any sense," she told her mother. "It's not like Jasmyn's dancing with us."

But I wanted her to, I thought to myself.

"Oh!" Mrs. Harrison put a hand to her mouth with a tiny gasp. "Do you think it would make her feel bad because she can't dance?"

"No!" I practically shouted. "I think she'd love it!"

"Really?" Mrs. Harrison brightened.

"Really!" I nodded as enthusiastically as I could. "It's a great idea!" *It was too perfect.* I thought, rubbing my hands together. *I could secretly rehearse with Jasmyn and then she could join us at the performance—complete with matching shoes!* "You're awesome, Mrs. Harrison."

"Why, thank you!" Mrs. Harrison fanned herself with her hand and fluttered her eyelashes.

I giggled and turned to grin at Rani, but instead of smiling back at me, Rani rolled her eyes as she yanked open the back door of her mother's car.

What's up with her? I wondered as I followed her into the car and buckled myself in. Mrs. Harrison continued to chat with me about the party as Rani stared out the window, ignoring both of us.

Mrs. Harrison caught a glimpse of her daughter in the rear-view mirror. "Tired, honeypie?" she asked.

"I guess," Rani said.

But I knew it was more than that. *I'll ask her tomorrow,* I decided. *Something is definitely bothering her.*

The next day I spent the whole morning before school wondering how and when I could ask Jasmyn if she was even interested in dancing again—without the others overhearing us. But my opportunity came up in a way I didn't expect.

After Ms. Roderick took attendance (this time her earrings were shaped like tiny stacks of pancakes—complete with melting pats of butter and cascading syrup) she clapped her hands to get our attention. "All right, class," she said. "Since last month we were all *reading* biographies, *this* month we're going to start *writing* them." Then, seeing the shocked expressions on our faces, she clarified, "Oh! Don't worry. I don't expect you to write *books.* Just essays. And the little biographies you are going to write will be . . ." she crossed her arms and pointed to either side of herself, ". . . all about your neighbor."

She began walking from one end of the "U" arrangement of desks and pairing up writers. "You will each take turns asking each other the interview questions. You'll find them right up there on the white board. You will write down each other's answers and those will be the notes that you will use to write the biographies."

When she got to our table she nodded and said to me and Jasmyn, "You two." (That meant that we were to interview each other.) The she kept walking. "You should fill two sides of a sheet of notebook paper. I'll be passing out handouts with a sample essay in the style and length I'm looking for."

June raised her hand.

"Yes, June?"

"Isn't it going to get awfully loud in here with all of us talking?"

"Good point," Ms. Roderick said. "Try talking softly to each other. But I want you to have real conversations with your neighbor. I think it's very important for children today to speak face-to-face instead of through screens all the time. Real human contact and understanding of other people is what's needed in this world."

As Jasmyn and I faced one another, we wriggled in our chairs with excitement.

"This is going to be fun!" Jasmyn said, rubbing her hands together. "I love anything to do with writing."

"Me, too!" I was happy to know that we shared something else in common.

"In fact," Jasmyn declared, "I want to be a writer when I grow up."

"Me, too!" I laughed. "Well, that, and a surgeon."

Jasmyn goggled at me. "What? Are you serious?"

"Mm-hm. My uncle's a surgeon. He's a general surgeon. And that's what I want to be. You can operate on lots of different parts of the body when you're a general surgeon. And you can help so many people. Especially in emergency situations."

"Wow," Jasmyn said. She was silent for a moment. Then she said, "You must be super-smart."

I shrugged. "Thanks." I glimpsed up at the white board. "Hey! We already covered one of the questions! 'What do you want to be when you grow up?' And I know the answer to that one already too: "What's your favorite color?'" I wrote 'orange' in bold letters on my loose-leaf paper.

"And yours is pink, right?" Jasmyn asked me.

"Yup! And I know the one after that: 'Do you have a hobby you enjoy?'" I raised my pencil in the air. "Knitting! And crocheting, of course!"

"And *you*," Jasmyn said, "love dancing!"

And there it was. The perfect opening.

"Yes, that's right," I said, watching her write in her tiny, neat handwriting. I cleared my throat. "Didn't you tell me that you used to dance?"

"Uh-huh."

"Did you like it?"

"Oh, yeah. Lots. I loved it. But . . ." a shadow seemed to fall across her face, "when my legs stopped doing what I wanted them to, I kind of lost interest. And now I just concentrate on doing other things that I'm good at."

I took a deep breath. "Did I tell you about what my dance teacher did the other day? Her name is Ms. Mandy and she hurt her ankle. Anyway, she needs a wheelchair for a while because she's not supposed to put pressure on it. So, what do you think she did? She taught our class *from* the wheelchair!"

Jasmyn's eyebrows shot up. "She did?"

"Yeah! And she was good too. I mean, she didn't use her legs, but she used her arms and upper body and face. She turned her wheelchair this way and that . . . She really danced! She told a story with her body and everything. She was great!"

Jasmyn blinked hard. "Really?"

"Yeah. You know what? It got me thinking. I thought that you could still dance if you wanted to. It would be different than you used to do it, but . . ."

Jasmyn said nothing. She just looked off to the side, like she was really thinking about it.

Then I blurted, "You should join The Ruby Slippers! I could teach you the routine and—"

That snapped Jasmyn to attention. "Oh, no, no, no, no, no, no!" she crisscrossed her hands and waved them in front of her face. "I couldn't do that! Not after all the problems you told me you had and everything! And you've all danced that choreography together before. I'd be joining you all so late. Plus, I'd have to learn it all from a wheelchair . . . no way. That'd be nuts."

"Okay! Okay! I didn't mean . . . it's just . . ." I sagged in my chair and said in a small voice, "I bet you can still dance." I shrugged. "Sorry."

"Don't be sorry," Jasmyn said with a half-smile. "I like that you think that."

"In fact," I said, "I still think you can totally do The Ruby Slippers dance if I taught it to you. In fact, . . . what if I *did* teach it to you? For fun? Would you like to learn it?"

Jasmyn said nothing, but the way she tilted her head made her look like she was thinking about it.

"If you don't want to join us on stage, I understand," I said. "In fact, we don't even have to tell any of the others that we're even doing this. It can be just you and me. What do you think? Do you want to give it a try?"

"Just you and me . . . ? Well . . ." Jasmyn raised her head to look at me, her cheeks pink and her eyes shining. "Okay then. Sure. Why not? Yes! Let's give it a try!"

Chapter 13

"So, when are we going to practice?" I whispered to Jasmyn when we were on our way to the cafeteria.

"Can you come over to my place after school tomorrow? I'll ask my parents tonight and you can ask your dad. Amber can come, too, if she wants."

"Okay! Let's—oh, hi, Rani!" I said suddenly when I noticed her coming down the hallway toward us. I nudged Jasmyn to let her know that we needed to stop talking about our plans since they were basically a secret.

Rani noticed the nudge, though, and frowned. "Why are you guys whispering?" she asked. "What's the big secret?"

I didn't know what to say. I looked at Jasmyn and then back at Rani. "Oh, it's nothing. Don't worry about it."

"Yes, it's nothing," Jasmyn echoed. But then she grinned.

This just made Rani frown more deeply. "If it's 'nothing' then why won't you tell me what it is?"

"Because it's nothing you need to know about," I said. I waved my hand, hoping that the move would wave away some of her worry. It didn't work.

Instead, her nostrils flared. "That's rude!" She hugged her schoolbooks close to her chest.

"So is asking about other people's private conversations," I pointed out before I could stop myself.

Rani widened her eyes, spun on her heel, and stomped away.

Sometimes I was too straightforward for my own good. "Rani," I called after her. "Sorry! Rani! Come back!"

But she kept walking.

Jasmyn was no longer smiling. She looked very serious. Scared even. "Ooh, she's mad."

"It'll be okay. She'll be at the lunch table. You'll see," I said. "I can apologize to her there."

But when we got to the lunch table, Rani wasn't there. June wasn't either. And even after Mariska, Quinn, Amber, Jasmyn, and I all started eating, Rani and June were still no-shows. So I explained to the others how I had hurt Rani's feelings earlier.

"Rani's probably around here somewhere." Amber squinted as she searched the cafeteria. Then she pointed. "There she is! She's with June! They're sitting together all the way at the other end!"

"Excuse me," I said, pushing back my chair. "I'm going to fix this."

As I approached their table, I could tell that June saw me coming and that she whispered this to Rani. I could also tell that Rani was making an effort not to turn around and watch me approach. I grabbed a nearby chair, pulled it up to their table, and sat myself down.

"Look, Rani, I'm sorry I was rude and hurt your feelings. I shouldn't have spoken to you that way. Come to the table and eat with the rest of us, please."

Rani still didn't turn to look at me. She just bit into her sandwich but kept the sandwich in her mouth while tears glistened in her eyes.

This made my heart hurt. "Oh, Rani! I said I am sorry!" I reached out and put a hand on one of her shoulders.

Rani shook her head. "I know," she said. She chewed the piece of her egg salad sandwich for a bit before talking again. "But you still didn't tell me what your big secret is."

Still wanting it to be a surprise, I hung my head. "But . . . my secret isn't bad. It's not really that much of a secret. It's more like a private thing. But it's not something that is supposed to hurt you. I wish you wouldn't let it."

Rani sniffed loudly. "I can't help it. Mom and Dad are always whispering these days. And now you and Jasmyn are too. I can't stand it." She began taking more bites out of her sandwich even though she hadn't finished chewing or swallowing the others. She was really stuffing her face.

I popped open her water bottle for her. *She's really going to need to wash that all down,* I thought as I handed it to her. "Do you think your parents have already decided if you're going to London or not?"

"No." Rani took the bottle and gulped a few times. "And I keep telling them that I really want to stay home with all my friends and keep going to this school." She wiped her eyes with a napkin. "Other times . . . when I stop to think about it . . . I think going to London could be really cool."

June sighed loudly.

Rani saw her and nodded. "And that scares me."

"You're scared of . . . London?" I asked.

"No. I'm scared that if I think about it being cool, then I might cause it to happen. And I'll *have* to move, and I'll be sorry."

"It's not like you have magic powers," I said reaching for a French fry that was on June's plate. June nodded, so I took it. "You can't *make* it happen. But still, I get what you mean. When my sisters and I moved here we were both happy and sad about it too. We left a lot of family and all of our friends behind, and the only home we'd ever known . . ." When I saw tears begin to glimmer in Rani's eyes again, I quickly added, ". . . but our new house is great, and so are our new friends, and family comes to visit us all the time."

"If we moved, it wouldn't exactly be to another state. It's a whole other country. Visiting would be a lot harder."

"That's true. So let's try to stop that move from happening and make sure we do a great job with the dance, okay?" I squirmed in my seat and looked over my shoulder. "Can we go back to our regular table, please?"

Rani crumpled her lunch bag. "Yeah, okay."

When Rani came back to the table, our friends cheered. This seemed to cheer her up. And it made me feel better too. That is, until I noticed that for the rest of our meal, Rani looked at and spoke to everyone—except Jasmyn.

Is it my imagination, I wondered, *or is Rani doing that on purpose?*

But I didn't get any more time to wonder, because at that moment, Mariska jumped up and said, "Come on, guys! We have some rehearsing to do!"

"No ballet this time!" I shouted after her. Then I glanced at Amber and Jasmyn. "Are you coming?"

"I wanted another crocheting lesson, actually," Amber said with a sneaky smile.

"Come on, now." I clucked my tongue. "That's not fair! She's going to be so far ahead!"

"No, she's not," Jasmyn said. "Did you get to watch any of the video that she took yesterday?"

"I did," I admitted. "Before bed. Only I couldn't practice any of it. I didn't have any needles or yarn."

Jasmyn clapped a hand over her forehead. "Oops! I should have thought of that! I wonder if I can give you something to take home today . . ."

"Actually," I said, trying to give Jasmyn a meaningful look, "I was hoping you could use my phone to take some video of our rehearsal right now. That way we—I mean, I—can look at the video later and practice to it." Then I added in a whisper, "*If* you know what I mean."

"Oooh," Jasmyn said. "Okay. Sure, I'll video it for you."

Amber groaned. "There goes my crocheting lesson!"

The next day was Friday—the day Rani's dad was supposed to make his decision. I could see that Rani *was* really nervous. All day long. For instance, whenever Ms. Roderick called on her, she would be staring into space. Ms. Roderick would sometimes have to call her name at least three times. One time Rani got up from her desk and knocked her pencil case over. Everything spilled out of it and rolled onto the floor. And at lunchtime, instead of stuffing her face, she could barely eat a thing.

The rest of us at the lunch table were nervous just seeing how nervous she was.

"When will your parents let you know?" I asked the question that everyone wanted the answer to.

"I don't know," Rani said, stirring her peas absentmindedly. "Sometime after Dad comes home, I guess. He isn't usually back until after six."

"Well, let us know what happens, okay?" I said.

Rani flashed me her teeth in a failed attempt at a smile. "Sure."

At the end of the school day, Rani was the first one outside. I wanted to follow her, but instead walked by Jasmyn's side since I was going to go home with her that afternoon.

I found Rani craning her neck, looking out into the line of cars that were pulling up in front of school. I could tell she was trying to spot her mother's car. Although she was standing in place, she was jiggling her legs nervously.

"Are you okay?" I asked. I walked up to her side and gave her a pat on the back.

Rani nodded "yes" but I didn't think she was. Then she began to say, "Will you . . . ?" but she stopped herself when she noticed Jasmyn on my other side.

"Will I what?" I asked.

"Oh . . . nothing."

I wanted to stay standing next to her and wait for her mother too. I wanted to see how Mrs. Harrison looked when she showed up. Would she appear sad? Excited? Or the same as always? Had Rani's parents made their decision?

Instead, Jasmyn's mother, Mrs. Wright, pulled up in front of us first. "Hi, girls!" She stepped out from behind the front wheel and waved at us cheerfully. Then she opened the side door of the van and activated its chair lift. "I understand that Amber is going to have a daddy-daughter day today," she said to me. "Is that right?"

"Yeah, I forgot about it. Dad takes all of us Daniels sisters out for some daddy-daughter time. He tries to give us each a day out with him once a month. Mom used to do that too.

They couldn't cancel today because they already had tickets to a flower show."

"Oh, I wouldn't want Amber to cancel her daddy-daughter day," Mrs. Wright said. "She can come over some other time. I'm glad you could come, though." She stepped inside the van to buckle Jasmyn's wheelchair into place.

"Me, too," I said.

Suddenly I got that feeling of being stared at. I turned my head to see Rani looking open-mouthed at both me and Jasmyn.

"You're going over to her place today?" she asked, blinking fast.

"Um, yeah."

"Now it's your turn," Mrs. Wright gestured for me to sit in a special seat next to Jasmyn's wheelchair.

I waved at Rani. "Gotta go. See you tomorrow. Call me later if you find out anything!"

Rani said nothing. She just turned away from me to stare out into the distance, like she was still looking for her mother's car.

"I don't think she heard you," Jasmyn said as I buckled into my seat.

But I was pretty sure she had.

When we got to Jasmyn's sunshine-filled home, I shouted, "This is so cool!" and my worries about Rani flew out of my head. Since the house was specially designed to make it easier for a person in a wheelchair to get around, I had fun noticing all the details that made it different from my place. I had to ask, "Can I take a video to show to my sisters?"

"Of course!" Mrs. Wright said.

As Jasmyn and her mother led me around in a tour of each room, I noticed that the house was only one story (not three, like mine) and that it was all spread out. So even though my own house was roomy, this house was even roomier, with furniture pieces set further apart from one another than most homes I'd seen before. It's *to make more space for the chair to move around,* I realized. There were no rugs or carpets—or even a lot of doors. And there were rounded corners on all the walls and furniture—no sharp edges. The whole place seemed open and airy. Even, I thought, a little space-agey.

Mrs. Wright led us to the kitchen. "Let me fix you girls a snack," she said.

"I'll get the glasses," Jasmyn said, following after her.

That's when I noticed that the kitchen cabinets all hung lower than they were at my house. This made it easier for Jasmyn to reach them. I filmed her as she opened a cabinet door and carefully pulled down an extendable shelf stocked with cups and glasses. After looking them over, she chose a pink glass and an orange glass. She placed the orange one in the cup holder on the side of her chair. She kept the pink one her hand. Then she brought them both to the counter.

"Thanks," I said. Then, noticing that even the microwave was set beneath the counter, I filmed it too, and said. "You have a really neat kitchen." I couldn't wait to show my sisters how cool everything in the house looked.

After a snack of chocolate chip cookies and milk, Jasmyn showed me to her room.

Since in the kitchen everything had been lower than I expected, I was surprised to find that her bed was higher than I expected. "It's supposed to be as high as my chair seat," she explained. "That way I can kind of just scoot into bed instead of pulling myself up or dropping myself down."

"Of course!"

What I liked best about her room was the hanging chair. It was made out of wicker and rope, and it dangled from the ceiling. With its egg shape and its orange cushions, it looked like it was part-swing, part Easter basket. "Sooo pretty!" I gushed. I panned the camera from the ceiling to the floor. "I think all my sisters will want one of these!"

When I was done filming the house, I searched my phone for the video file of The Ruby Slippers' rehearsal from the day before.

"Thanks for filming this," I said. "I'll give you a copy of this file so you can practice to it when you are alone. But in the meantime," I propped the phone up on a nearby bookshelf, "let's go over the arm movements first."

As I showed Jasmyn what to do, I was impressed with how quickly she picked up on the choreography. Sometimes she was even ahead of me. "Then I'm supposed to do something like this, right? And then . . . something like . . . ?"

"Exactly! Wow!" I shook my head in amazement. "You're much faster at remembering choreography than I am."

Jasmyn giggled, sounding partly embarrassed and partly pleased by the praise. "I like learning choreography," she admitted. "And I like this dance. But you know what dance I really like?" she asked shyly. "Yours!"

"Mine?"

"The one Amber showed me on her phone. I especially liked when you did this . . . and this . . ." And right in front of my eyes Jasmyn began using her arms like I had in my "God is Good" dance.

My mouth fell open. "I *did* do that! You remembered! And you only saw it once."

"I thought it looked really good," Jasmyn said. "You know, I hope this doesn't make you mad or anything, but I'd rather learn *that* dance than this one."

"Really?" I was a little disappointed that she didn't want to learn the Ruby Slippers dance, because that meant that she wouldn't be joining us on stage. At the same time, I was amazed that she preferred my dance instead.

"I can teach it to you," I said. "I mean, we'll have to change it around so that it's a duet and work out ways to include your wheelchair." I suddenly began imagining all the little changes I would need to do to the dance. But it was exciting to have so many ideas. "The only problem is we won't be able to perform it at the talent show," I told her.

"That's okay," Jasmyn said. "I just want to learn the dance. I don't need to be in the talent show."

"Good," I said. But I sighed sadly as I stopped the video on the phone.

"What's the matter?" Jasmyn asked. "Are you mad at me?"

"What? No!" I sat down on the bed and told her about my failed attempt to sign up for the talent show to dance to "God Is Good."

"So, as you can see, I'm still pretty bummed about that," I admitted.

"Yeah," Jasmyn said. "But you said that there's a chance a space could open, right?" She suddenly looked nervous.

"Well, yeah."

"Then you'll need to practice. You'll need to practice as much as you would if you were sure you had a spot. To be ready, just in case."

"I guess."

"Then forget about trying to teach me the dance," Jasmyn said. "It'll just confuse you."

I stood up and crossed my arms. "I'll do no such thing. Besides, I have too many cool ideas for the dance crowding my head now." I began searching my phone for the music file of "God Is Good."

"If I do get a slot in the talent show to dance to 'God Is Good,'" I said, pressing play. "I'll only want to do it if you do it with me. Okay?"

"Really?" Jasmyn stared up at me, her eyes large behind her glasses.

"Really. Are you ready to begin?" I stepped out the middle of the room and began to dance.

We spent a good chunk of the afternoon learning the dance together (because I was making up new choreography). After a while she had to play the music on her computer so that we could film one another (and us together) on our phones. By the time we finished up our practice we had some of the moves down. At the end, she even spun in her chair at the same time I turned. We began and ended the spin at the exact same time!

"This is really going to work!" I said, panting. "We work well together."

"The music helps a lot too," Jasmyn explained. "I move when it tells me. And I also really love the words to the song. I feel them in my heart. You know what I mean?"

I nodded as I sat myself in the hanging chair. "Yeah, I do. Whenever I hear that beginning about getting bad news, I think about when my mom died."

"And I think about when my parents told me I was going to

lose my ability to walk," Jasmyn confessed. "Just like the song says, I didn't know what to do."

"Me neither," I said, swinging lightly in the chair. "But you know how in the song it says that the mother would say to praise God? That's exactly what my mom would say. Praise Him no matter what, because God is good even when things are bad."

"Check out that pillow tucked behind you," Jasmyn said.

I yanked an orange pillow out from behind my back and flipped it over. There was a needlepoint design of a shaded path on it and the words, "Trust in the Lord with all your heart and lean not on your own understanding—Proverbs 3:5" stitched across it.

I gasped. "Did you make this?"

"No," Jasmyn chuckled. "But I do want to get that good at stitching." She rolled over to look at the pillowcase more closely. "I just pointed it out because the song kind of reminds me of this Scripture. When I first heard that I would be needing a wheelchair I used to sleep with this pillow under my head."

"So you didn't lean on your own understanding," I said. "You leaned on this pillow."

"You're right!" Jasmyn laughed.

I hopped off the chair. "I *do* trust God," I said, "but I miss my mom too. I really wish she could be here to see me and Amber in the talent show."

"But she will see you. Don't you think she can see you from heaven? She'll watch your performance and be so proud."

I pictured my mother doing just that and I knew Jasmyn was right. "Okay, then," I said. "I guess that means we need to practice our act some more. I want us to look good for Mom."

"I want to look good for your mom too," Jasmyn said.

I put the music on again. "Let's start at the top."

We went over the whole song one more time before we stopped. This time it was because when we turned together, we found Mrs. Wright standing in the doorway.

"Oh, hi, Mom—" Jasmyn began. "Wait. What's wrong?"

Mrs. Wright had tears in her eyes.

Chapter 14

"What are you two doing?" Mrs. Wright asked. Her voice sounded a little high-pitched and quivery.

"Dancing," we said at the same time.

"That's what I thought!" Mrs. Wright clasped her hands together. "Oh! It's so nice to see you dancing again, Jasmyn!"

So, they were happy tears. *Phew.*

"Yeah . . ." Jasmyn said, "well, it's *fun!*" She explained to her mother that I was teaching her a dance I had choreographed to "God Is Good." She didn't mention the talent show because we didn't really know if we'd get the chance to be in it. Besides, we hadn't finished figuring out how the whole dance would go yet.

Jasmyn swayed her wheelchair from side to side to side playfully. "Ashton takes dance class at a place called . . . what's it called again, Ashton?"

"Tambourine Studios," I told Mrs. Wright. "It's a great place."

Mrs. Wright looked thoughtful. "I'll have to see if I can sign Jasmyn up for some classes there. Would you like that, Jasmyn?"

"Oh, yes!" Jasmyn clapped her hands. "Thank you, Mommy!"

We practiced a little while longer after that. Then I helped her put together the knitting needles, crochet hooks, and balls of yarn she was going to take to my place on Sunday. She also showed me a few other things she had crocheted, like hats, scarves, and the throw she had laying across her bed.

"Ooh, I can't wait to get started!" I said, placing a fat ball of rainbow-colored yarn in a special backpack built to go on the back of a wheelchair. "Can you teach me something now? Show me what you showed Amber? I want to know as much as she knows before the party!"

"Okay!" Jasmyn laughed. She unrolled a special yellow velvet pouch filled with all kinds knitting needles and hooks. Most of them were metal, but some were made of wood, and others something else. Like a plastic or something. They were many different sizes too. After looking them over carefully, she slid a couple of shiny hooks out. "Tell me," she said with a shy smile, "Do you and Amber always compete with each other?"

"No," I said. "Not exactly." I felt a little warm around the neck. "It's not about being in a contest with one another. It's more about being even-steven. You know, being fair. I mean, we're *twins*."

"But you guys don't need to do *everything* the same," Jasmyn said. "Right? You dance, she sings. You're here now, she's with your dad. . . ."

I shrugged. "We *don't* have to do everything the same," I agreed. "Except for *some* things—like crocheting!"

Jasmyn giggled. "So do the two of you fight a lot?"

"Yeah," I admitted. "But we have a lot of fun together too."

Jasmyn sighed. "You guys are so lucky." She held out some balls of yarn for me to choose from. "It must be nice to have sisters."

"It is," I said choosing a ball of pretty coral pink yarn. "I love my sisters. I really do. We can drive each other crazy. But when we work together, we can be a real team. So, yeah, we're lucky. Except Dad would say, 'Not lucky—blessed.' So we're blessed!"

"You know what being blessed means?" Jasmyn had a twinkle in her eye.

"What . . . ?"

"That you have reasons to . . . " and she started singing, ". . . sing praises to the Lord . . . !"

I joined in. ". . . for God is good!"

When I got home later that evening, I put my hands on my hips and looked around my house with new eyes.

"Not bad, not bad," I said. "But," I explained to my family at dinner time, "we're going to have to make sure this place is more wheelchair-friendly before Jasmyn visits on Sunday. You'll see what I mean when I show you the video I took of her place."

"Making this place more wheelchair-friendly sounds like a good little project we can work on tomorrow," Aunt Sam said.

Ansley and Lena agreed.

Aunt Sam took a pizza cutter out of a drawer in the kitchen and sliced into the homemade pizza pie she had taken out of the oven minutes earlier. "We'll also have to do some shopping for the party. I'll need you girls to come along to help me choose things at the market."

"Okay," Lena said as she set the table.

"No problem." Ansley nodded.

"But I've got dance," I said.

"I'll pick you up after, and then we'll swing over to the store." Aunt Sam slid a slice of pizza onto a dish and handed it to me.

Just then, Dad and Amber came through the front door.

"Sorry we're late," Dad called out as he peeled off his jacket in the entry way. "Friday traffic."

Amber trotted into the kitchen, smiling widely. She was holding a small potted plant with both her hands. "Isn't it pretty?" she asked all of us. She set it down on the counter and took off her sweater. "You'll never guess what it is."

I had just taken a bite of my pizza slice, and a melty string of cheese still connected my mouth to the slice. So, holding the slice in one hand and the plate in the other, I carefully made my way over to take a closer look. Ansley and Lena also gathered around the plant with its shiny, dark green leaves and tiny white flowers.

"Hmm," Lena said. "Smells like perfume."

"I know what it is," I said. But with the pizza in my mouth it sounded more like, "I nub wuh eh iz." I pulled the cheese string into my mouth, chewed, and swallowed. "A jasmine plant!"

"Yes!" Amber looked amazed that I knew. "We're going to give this to Jasmyn's parents as a housewarming gift."

"Great idea!" I said.

"I was just telling the girls that I'll need their help with the grocery shopping tomorrow." Aunt Sam told Dad. "We'll go after Cammie's dance class."

"But Cammie's supposed to go to Rani's afterwards for some talent show rehearsal," Dad reminded her. "It's on the calendar."

"Oh, right. But that's just for an hour. Okay. We'll just pick her up from there."

Dad walked over to the calendar that we had hanging on the kitchen wall and looked it over. "Today was the day Rani's dad was supposed to make his decision," he announced. "Any news on that, yet, Cam?"

I dropped my pizza onto my plate. "That's right. No, I haven't heard anything." Suddenly I felt jittery inside. I placed my plate on the table and pushed it away. "Should I call her?"

"No. Let her call you," Dad said, accepting the slice of pizza his sister offered him. "Or just ask her tomorrow when you see her at dance."

"Okay." I nodded.

Dad leaned over to look me in the eyes. "You okay?"

"I'm just a little worried that it's not good news," I said.

Dad patted me on the arm. "Well, you know what they say, 'No news is good news.'"

"I never really got that," I said. "Why exactly do people say that again?"

Taking time to think and chew, Dad looked up to the side. Then he turned back to me and said, "I think they mean that when it's bad news people will get in touch with you to let you know. But when all is well, there's no news to tell, so people don't reach out. So, if you haven't heard anything, that's probably because it's all good."

Hearing that made me feel better. But then another idea came into my mind. "Of course, Rani may not have called me because she's too upset to speak."

Lena shook her head. "Now you sound like me! You're worrying too much."

"And what did your mom and I tell you about worrying, Lena?"

Lena scooted her chair closer to me. "She told me to read certain Scriptures in the Bible for comfort. Like the lilies of the field reading in Matthew chapter 6, verse 27, 'Can any of you by worrying add a single hour to your life?' and verse 33: 'Seek first his kingdom and his righteousness.' and verse 34: 'Therefore do not worry about tomorrow, for tomorrow will worry about itself.'"

"And what about Proverbs chapter 3, verse 5? 'Trust in the Lord . . .'" Dad began.

"'. . . and lean not on your own understanding,'" I finished, remembering Jasmyn's pillow.

"Very good!" Dad said approvingly. "Whatever happens, just remember that God is in charge and he knows what is best for Rani and her parents. Just put your worries in God's hands. Okay?"

"Okay," I said.

When Dad and Amber started talking about the flower show, I took a moment to close my eyes and imagine putting Rani and her parents in a giant pair of hands. God's hands. The hands curled up around them and held them securely. *It's all going to be okay,* I told myself. *God's got this.*

After breakfast on Saturday morning but before dance class, I met with my sisters in the living room while Aunt Sam got some laundry started upstairs.

"Okay," I said, clapping my hands together. "You all saw the video. Now we need to make this place more wheelchair-friendly. What are some ways we can do this?"

"Maybe we can imagine ourselves in wheelchairs," Amber said, "and go all around the house looking for places where we might run into problems . . . or something."

"All around the ground floor, anyway," Lena said. "We don't have a way to bring her upstairs."

"That's a bummer," I said, realizing I wouldn't be able to show Jasmyn my room.

"I got it!" Ansley leapt in the air. "We don't have to imagine ourselves in a wheelchair . . . we can get a chair with wheels!" She dashed out of the room.

Amber, Lena, and I all looked at each other and then ran after her.

We found Ansley in Dad's office, rolling his chair out from under his desk.

"What are you doing? That's Dad's," Lena said. "We should ask him first."

"But he's out. Besides, I'm just," Ansley grunted, "borrowing it." She waved us away from the open French doors so that she could push the chair through them. "It's for a good cause."

"Oooh, I get it," Amber said. "You want to push that chair around the house and see if there's room for it to move."

Ansley nodded.

"And to see if the wheels have any problems rolling over places," I added with understanding.

"Exactly!" Ansley rolled the chair out into the foyer beside the front door. "Open the door," she told Lena, "and let's start like she's entering the house." She sat in the chair. "I'll be Jasmyn. Somebody push me."

"Wait a minute, wait a minute," I said. "I should be Jasmyn. She's *my* friend."

"She's my friend too," Amber said in a quiet voice.

"Besides," I went on, "Jasmyn doesn't have anyone push her wheelchair for her," I said. "She controls it herself with a joystick."

"Yeah, but in case you haven't noticed," Ansley motioned

in the air above the armrests, "no joysticks here. Besides, her wheelchair's heavier than this chair, so I just wanted to weigh this chair down a little."

"Then Lena should sit on it," I said. "She's the oldest and the biggest. You're a gymnast and light as a feather."

"But," Ansley argued, "Jasmyn's small too. She's only ten!"

"But," Lena broke in, "you just said her wheelchair was heavy!"

"Her chair is kind of small, actually," I said. "And not that heavy." When we had rehearsed our dance the day before she had told me that her chair was considered lightweight, and only about forty pounds or so.

"We're wasting time," Ansley said, gripping the armrests with frustration. "Let's just get this done. It doesn't matter who is in the chair."

"If it doesn't matter," I said, "then I can sit in it."

"Oh, fine!" Ansley got up from the chair and I took her place.

"Okay," I said, "let's roll!"

Even after our bickering, we Daniels sisters took our job very seriously. We took great care in making sure that a wheelchair could make its way around all the rooms on the ground floor (not to mention from the driveway to the front door). And even though the desk chair was in no way a perfect substitute for Jasmyn's power chair, it still helped us to figure out how to make sure there was enough space and smooth paths for her when she made her visit.

When we were done, we carefully put Dad's chair back where it belonged. Then we walked directly across the hall to the formal dining room. It was where we decided our crocheting lesson was going to be. There was room enough there for all of us to sit around and to be able to see Jasmyn when she showed us what to do. Plus, we could put all of our yarn and supplies on the table.

"Jasmyn can sit here," Lena said, pointing to a space at the head of the table. "We'll just move this chair to the side. We can even bring some more chairs from the kitchen if we have to."

"I can hardly wait until tomorrow." Amber smiled her dimpled smile. "It's going to be such fun!"

"And delicious, too, don't forget," Ansley added. "With my heart-shaped cinnamon rolls."

My mouth watered at the thought. "Yeah!" I said. "Rani loves those too—" I stopped. I'd be seeing Rani soon. I wondered what news she would have to tell me.

Just then, we heard Aunt Sam coming down the stairs. "I hope you're dressed and ready, Cammie, because it's time to take you to Tambourine," she said. She grabbed the keys from the bowl in the entryway.

I waved at my sisters.

"We hope Rani has good news!" Lena said. "Bye!"

Chapter 15

The drive to Tambourine was only ten minutes, but it felt way longer than that. And I kept looking to see if I could find Rani's car on the road on the way, but I didn't. When we got to Tambourine, I checked the parking lot and the front desk area for Rani, too, but still nothing. *I sure hope she's in the locker room already,* I thought as I let myself in.

She was there.

Surrounded by friends.

And smiling.

I breathed a sigh of relief. "So, you're staying?"

At the sound of my voice (which kind of echoed in the locker room), Rani, Mariska, June, and Quinn all turned to look at me. Rani's smile fell and she hung her head.

I gasped. "You're going?"

"Actually," she said looking down at her fingernails. "I don't know yet. My father got a few extra days to make his decision. He'll have to let them know on Monday."

"Then we still won't know for three more days?" It was too hard for me to hide my disappointment. "Ugh!" I made a face and sat down hard on a nearby bench.

"Yeah, I know," Rani said. "But I overheard Mom talking to Dad last night. It sounded like she was trying to get him to let us stay." Her eyes lit up. "She even said, 'We have to let

Rani perform at the show,' and 'All of her friends want her to stay.'"

"Yeah, well, your mom was right. We do all want you to stay. That's why we're doing this dance in the first place, right?"

"Right," Rani said.

"I wish you had called me last night or something," I told her as I began to untie my sneakers. "I was worried when I didn't hear from you."

"Were you?" Rani raised her eyebrows. "I thought you were too busy with Jasmyn to worry about me."

"Actually, I didn't really worry about you when I was at her place," I told Rani truthfully. "But I did around dinner time when I figured your Dad would be home to tell you his decision."

"Why were you over at Jasmyn's anyway?" Rani asked, wrinkling her nose.

"Huh?" I dropped my second sneaker with a thud. "Why do you think? Because she invited me."

"Oh. Well, no. It's just that you two seem to be together all the time these days."

"She is my school buddy," I said. "And now she's my friend too."

"That's fine of course," Rani said. "And it's nice that you're friends. I just wanted to make sure you didn't still want her to be in our Ruby Slipper dance because," she looked around at the other girls who all gave her tiny nods before she continued, "it wouldn't be very fair to add her to our dance after we all said 'no' and everything."

My ears and cheeks burned hot with both embarrassment and anger. If Jasmyn hadn't decided on her own that she didn't want to be a member of The Ruby Slippers I would have been in big trouble right then. At the same time, I couldn't stand how the other girls kept trying to keep Jasmyn out of the dance troupe. "You know," I said, standing up to face them as I put my hands on my hips, "you guys aren't being very Matthew 25-ish."

"What?" Rani put *her* hands on *her* hips. "What do you mean?"

"It's just that you guys don't seem very welcoming towards Jasmyn," I said. "I mean, the way you keep shutting her out."

"That's not true!" Rani huffed, although she didn't quite look me in the eye. "It's just that you said it yourself. The whole point of this Ruby Slipper dance is for me. To show my parents I'm needed here. That my friends want me to stay. You're my friend. And okay, you say she is yours. But is she really one of my friends, yet? I just met her. But if she's in the dance, then the dance will become all about *her* instead of *me.* The audience will be too busy noticing the girl in the wheelchair to pay attention to the rest of us." When she was finished speaking, Rani let out a long, hot breath.

I looked around at the other girls. They all looked uncomfortable, but as though they agreed with Rani.

"Well, you don't have to worry," I told them all as I crammed my dance bag into my locker with more force than was needed. "Just because Rani's mom is going to give her a pair of red slippers, it doesn't mean that Jasmyn is going to *be* a Ruby Slipper. Okay?" I slammed my locker shut.

I charged out of the locker room fuming. *Boy, do I wish another slot in the talent show would open up,* I thought to myself as we all headed out to the dance studio. *Then we'd show them all that Jasmyn doesn't need to have on red shoes or even be a Ruby Slipper to dance in the show!*

"Quick! Get in place, Ashton!" Ms. Mandy said, clapping from her wheelchair. "It's time to get started."

I kept thinking about what Rani said in the locker room and playing it over it in my head like one of my cell phone videos. It made it very hard for me to concentrate, and Ms. Mandy kept having to correct me. "No, Ashton, pay attention! Ashton, wake up, please. Ashton? Hello?"

When class was over, we all changed back into regular clothes pretty quickly. The other girls chatted more with each other than with me since they could see I was still angry. When we got to the reception area, we found Mrs. Harrison already waiting for us. Once she saw that we were all together she announced happily, "You'll never guess who I saw here not fifteen minutes ago! Jasmyn and her mom! Can you believe it?"

"Jasmyn? Here?" Rani asked, exchanging glances with Mariska. "At Tambourine?"

"Yes," Mrs. Harrison went on. "Her mom said something about you teaching her a dance, Ashton. The dance for the talent show or something? And how it's inspired them to sign her up for lessons at Tambourine too."

"That's . . . great," I said as I felt Rani's, Mariska's, June's, and Quinn's eyes all turn to look at me at the same time. It was like having four spotlights on me at once.

"Now I know that getting Jasmyn those red dance slippers is a good idea," Mrs. Harrison said turning to lead us out the door. "I told her mother about them. She said that Jasmyn will be thrilled!" She stopped short. "Oh, no! It looks like it's started to rain. You girls wait here under the awning. I'll go get the car and pull up to the front." She pulled a tiny umbrella from out of her purse and ran on tip-toe toward the parking lot.

Once she was gone, all the girls turned on me.

"You taught her our dance?" Rani said.

At the same time Mariska said, "You told her she could be in the talent show with us?"

And June said, "Even though we said 'no'?"

Even Quinn said, "You lied!"

I held up my hands. "Stop it! Stop it! It's not like that! She doesn't want to dance with the Ruby Slippers! Honest! And she's not going to be in the talent show with us!" I didn't want to admit that I originally *had* taught her the dance so that she could be in the talent show with us. Or that I was now teaching her my dance because she liked it better. "And so what if I taught her a few steps? So what if I told her she could dance in her wheelchair the way Ms. Mandy does? And what's wrong with her signing up for dance classes at Tambourine? I'll tell you what: nothing!"

The girls fell silent.

"You guys don't even hear how mean you sound," I said, and whirled around to point straight at Rani's chest. "What if you do end up moving to London? Do you want your new friends there to treat you the way you're treating Jasmyn? To be nice to your face but to say behind your back that they aren't really your friends? Do you want them to not want to include you in clubs and things? To not invite you over?"

I couldn't go on because at that point Rani burst into tears and her mother's car pulled up beside us.

Mrs. Harrison looked at us with wide eyes. "What happened? I was just gone for two minutes! Rani, what's wrong?"

Rani shook her head but continued to cry. After sighing deeply, Mrs. Harrison said, "Just get in the car, girls."

After buckling ourselves in, we all sat in awkward silence—except for the even more awkward sound of Rani sniffling every couple of minutes. Mrs. Harrison kept glancing in the rearview mirror to check on us. "Does anyone want to talk about it?"

"I think we're all just really tired," Mariska said.

"You girls have been very busy these days," Mrs. Harrison said, slowing down the speed on the windshield wipers. "You'll all feel better after you get something to eat. How do hot dogs, potato chips, and homemade lemonade sound to everyone?"

"MMmm!"

"Yum!"

"Yeah!"

"Great," I said.

Once we were at Rani's place, Mrs. Harrison shooed us away from the kitchen. "Why don't you show the girls your fish tank?" she suggested to Rani. She turned to Mariska and Quinn, who hadn't really seen the whole house the way June and I already had. "Wait until you see it. It's Mr. Harrison's pride and joy."

The fish tank was really a huge aquarium that took up the corner of Mr. Harrison's study.

It was filled with all sort of different colored fish that flicked around in the water, shining like little jewels. And it was decorated with many beautiful stones and plants, as well as a miniature scuba diver, a tiny treasure chest, and little cave the fish could swim through. Whenever I stopped to look at the aquarium, I liked to imagine a story about the scuba diver finding the old pirate's treasure in the cave! I loved that tank. But in the mood I was in, I didn't really want to see it. "Can I help you in the kitchen, Mrs. Harrison?" I asked.

"Are you sure, honey? You don't have to."

"Oh, no, I want to!" I insisted.

Mrs. Harrison put some hot dogs to boil as I set out the mustard, ketchup, dishes, and napkins on the dining room table. Then she cut up lemons and let me use her fancy countertop lemon juicer to make the lemonade. She also let me throw in the ice cubes—which weren't shaped like cubes at all, but diamonds instead.

I had so much fun helping her out. It reminded me of what it used to be like back when Rani and I first became friends and I started going to her house. Mrs. Harrison was always inviting us to help her around the kitchen. Once we even made a whole meal together of baked chicken, mashed potatoes, and string beans with a chocolate cheesecake for dessert.

If Rani moved away, I realized, I wouldn't only miss her, but her mother too.

After taking a pair of tongs out of a drawer, Mrs. Harrison began to pluck the hotdogs out of the hot water. "Go call the girls and tell them that lunch is ready," she said.

I swallowed hard. "Okay." I ran to Mr. Harrison's study where I found the girls all huddled together, speaking in low tones. "Um, lunch is ready," I said. "We're eating in the dining room because it's still raining."

"Thanks," Rani said.

As we ate our lunch, we all laughed and chatted as usual. You'd never know we'd had an argument half an hour before. I could see it made Mrs. Harrison happy to see us all getting along again. But the whole time I ate, I kept expecting the other girls to apologize to me or to say that they were sorry about how they had acted about Jasmyn. But instead, a couple of times I it seemed to me that they were expecting *me* to apologize to *them.*

When lunch was over Mrs. Harrison said she would put everything away. "Don't touch those dishes, Ashton!" she said. "You girls all need to get some practice in. Now go!"

We assembled in the family room and pushed back the furniture as usual. "Let's all wear our Ruby Slippers!" I suggested. After we slipped them on, I had to admit that I really loved the way our feet all matched. "They look great!" I said.

We practiced for twenty minutes. We all danced okay. Not great. All except Rani, who danced worst of all.

"Rani," I said, trying not to lose my patience after she made the wrong turn for the fourth time in a row. "Do you need a break?"

Rani stopped dancing, stomped over to the sofa and threw herself on it. "No, I don't need a break," she said. "I need to quit! I'm quitting the Ruby Slippers!"

Chapter 16

My heart began to pound hard and fast. "What?"

I shut the music off and we all stopped dancing to gather around Rani "You don't really mean that!" I said.

"Yes, I do!" Rani sat with her arms *and* legs crossed.

"But you *have* to be in the show," I reminded her. I dropped my voice to a whisper. "Otherwise your parents might not think you don't want to stay!"

Rani sat pouting.

"Rani! Do you want your parents to think you want to leave? Come on, don't quit now!"

"You could always join the Red Shoes instead," Mariska suggested.

"Oh, can I?" Rani's arms and legs slipped out of their pretzel-like poses. "Really?"

"Sure!"

"No, wait." I said. "You can't!"

"Why not?" Rani asked.

"Because . . . because . . . this whole thing was my idea! Entering the talent show! Dancing together! *My* idea."

"I know. But does it really matter if I'm in the Red Shoes or the Ruby Slippers as long as I get to dance with my friends in the talent show?" Rani asked.

"Well, yeah, because . . . because . . . well, for one, June is your friend and she's not in the Red Shoes," I pointed out.

Mariska looked over her shoulder. "Want to join us, June? You can if you want."

"Sure," June said.

This couldn't be happening. "But I'm also your friend," I said. "And I'm not in the Red Shoes, either."

"Well, that's kind of a problem," Mariska said. "I mean, I'd invite you to join us, but I know you wouldn't want to. You don't like dancing ballet, do you?"

"Well, no—"

"Then you wouldn't want to dance with us," Mariska said. "Trust me."

"Probably not, but—"

"We should really practice, you guys," Mariska told the others. She yanked her phone from out of her back pocket and scrolled through its music library until she found the classical instrumental piece she was looking for. She pressed "play."

"But what about The Ruby Slippers?" I asked over the sound of a full orchestra.

"We can practice some more at school on Monday," Mariska said.

"Just without *me*," Rani said. She got up from the couch and brushed past me to stand behind Mariska.

"Follow me, everyone," Mariska said, and she began dancing in a series of ballet moves and saying words in French that sounded like, "Ah-som-blay" and "bree-zay" and "sha-say".

It was my turn to throw myself down on the couch. I was in shock. *What just happened? How could Rani quit like that? How could all the girls just shut me out and go on dancing without me?*

"ASHTON!" Mrs. Harrison called out from the kitchen. "Your aunt is here! Says you have errands to run with her?"

The other girls barely looked at me when I leapt off the couch, whipped off my dancing shoes, and practically jumped into my sneakers. When I shouted "Bye!" to them over my shoulder, I didn't look back at them, either. I had never been so happy to leave Rani's house.

After saying good-bye to Mrs. Harrison, I ran out the front door toward my aunt's car. I could see that Lena, Ansley, and Amber were all with her.

I climbed inside next to Amber, covered my face with my hands, and didn't speak.

"Oh, no," Aunt Sam said. "I guess Rani is moving to London, huh?"

"No," I said. "But I wish she *would!*" Then it all tumbled out of me. When I got to the part when she quit The Ruby Slippers my sisters all gasped. And when I told them how Mariska wouldn't even invite me to be in the Red Shoes, they gasped again.

That is, all except Amber, who said, "Well, they know you don't like dancing ballet, so of course they wouldn't ask you—"

I glared at her until she stopped speaking.

"No doubt they were very rude to you," Aunt Sam said, steering the car out onto the road. At least it had stopped raining. "But from what you said, you had some rude moments yourself. It sounds like these are problems that can be fixed with some apologies from each side."

"I'm not so sure about that," I said. "I'm not even sure Rani wants to be my friend anymore." The lump in my throat felt like a sharp rock that was growing heavier and heavier.

"Of course she still wants to be your friend," Aunt Sam said. "You'll see, she'll come to the party tomorrow and so will all the other girls. In fact, the party will probably be the perfect place and time for everyone to apologize and make up with one another."

"Or," I muttered, "the time and place where everything will fall apart."

"Cammie," Aunt Sam said in a soothing voice, "you know as well as anyone that it can be hard to trust in God's goodness when things get tough. But that's exactly what God is calling you to do right now."

What she said made me think of Dad and how he'd told me to bring my problems to God and expect Him to take care of them. I sighed. "Right. Okay."

Aunt Sam pulled into the parking lot of the mall, shut off the car, and turned around in the driver's seat to face me. "It'll be okay, Cammie. You'll see," she said. "Rani's going through a lot of stress right now, but she'll come around. Let's go find something she'd like to eat at the party. After all, food," Aunt Sam said with a wink, "makes everyone happy."

The shopping trip ended up feeling like both work and fun. (We made sure Ansley had enough ingredients to make two batches of heart-shaped cinnamon rolls!) But with all the dancing and arguing and shopping and preparing for the party, I was exhausted by the time we got home. The second we were done putting all the groceries away, I dropped myself down in the nearest chair.

"Dinner will be ready in half an hour, okay?" Aunt Sam said.

I nodded. *Maybe I'll lie down for a few minutes,* I thought to myself, and headed for my room. But before I started up the staircase, I heard Dad call out for me and Amber. He was in his office.

Amber and I ran over before he had to call us twice. But he was smiling and pointing to his computer screen. "You have a call."

Amber and I ran over to either side of Dad, but he got up so that Amber and I could sit in it together while we talked to our friend, Giovanna.

Giovanna had been our neighbor and classmate when we lived in Texas. I remember her crying when she first heard that we had to move away. But now we video chatted with each other at least once a week to share what was happening in our lives.

"You know what?" Giovanna leaned closer to the camera in her excitement. Her whole face practically filled the screen. "Mom and Dad have signed me up for Camp Caracara already! Didn't we have a lot of fun there together last year?"

"Oh, yeah!" I said.

"It was great!" Amber agreed.

"What do you think if we could have fun there together *again*?" Giovanna asked. She raised an eyebrow. "Hint? Hint?"

"Wait. You mean ask Dad if we can go there, like, *this* summer?" I leaned in closer to the computer too.

"Back to Texas?" Amber added. She tilted her head as if to hear Giovanna better.

"Yes! That's exactly what I mean! I'd love to see you guys. And we'd have so much fun. It would be just for a couple of weeks. Wouldn't it be wonderful to be back together again? So, can you ask him? Please? Please?"

I loved the idea, and all I had to do was take one look at Amber to know that she did too. We nodded at each other. "Okay!" we promised. "We will!"

After chatting a little while longer, we said goodbye to Giovanna until next week, when it would be our turn to call her.

"And don't forget to ask your Dad about camp before you call me," Giovanna said before hanging up. "Then you can let me know what he says!"

But when we went looking for Dad afterwards, we heard him on the patio talking to someone on the phone.

"Let's just wait until tomorrow," I suggested to Amber as we made our way up the stairs. "After the party, when things have quieted down around here."

At that moment Aunt Sam called out, "Dinner's ready!" and accidently dropped the lid to an aluminum pot with a loud clatter. This set off the dogs, and they both began barking.

Amber laughed. "When things have quieted down around here?"

I had to laugh too.

That night, after I said my prayers and went to bed, I lay in the dark thinking about all that had happened that day. Then I began thinking about all that was going to happen tomorrow. When I realized I was worrying again, something Jesus said not to do, I crawled back out from under the covers, knelt by my bed, and said another prayer.

Dear God, I prayed in my mind, *Both Dad and Aunt Sam have told me to put my problems in your hands. Well, here is my problem. I'm worried that I might be losing my friend, Rani. In the beginning, I was afraid that if she moved to London, I would lose her that way. Now it looks like even if she doesn't move away, I will still lose her. Just in another way. And this way feels way worse because it's by her own choice.*

You want to know what else I'm worried about? I'm worried that Rani and the girls might not come to the party tomorrow. Or that if they do come to the party tomorrow, they won't treat Jasmyn well. And I'm worried about how it might make Jasmyn feel. Or what I might even say to them if I think they're being rude to her.

As you can see, I have a lot of worries, God. And I don't like it. It's not like me to be worried. So I'm giving them all to you. Please help me to trust you take care of how everything goes tomorrow. I ask this in Jesus' name, Amen.

After that prayer, I climbed back into bed feeling lighter and more relaxed. And before I knew it, I had a peaceful night's sleep.

The next morning, before church, we all ran around the house making sure everything was in order for the party later. We had to, because we would have no time to do so when we got home. The party would start right after Sunday school.

Rani, June, Mariska, and Quinn were not in our Sunday school class, though, which I was glad about. With all that happened yesterday, I didn't want the day to start with an argument or something. Instead, it was just me, Amber, and Jasmyn.

When Amber went to the bin to pick out her needlepoint project, I asked Jasmyn, "So how did it go at Tambourine yesterday?"

"Great!" Jasmyn said. "It turns out they are beginning a small class for kids in wheelchairs. I start next week."

"Cool!"

When class was over, it was finally time for the party. Because Jasmyn and her parents followed us home in their van, they were the first guests to arrive. We took them all around the rooms on the ground floor with the dogs yapping around us the whole time. At least the Wrights loved dogs, and the dogs didn't get in the way (much). Best of all, Jasmyn's chair had a really easy time making its way around from room to room. My sisters and I all noticed this and we quietly high-fived each other. We'd done a great job.

Soon the doorbell was ringing again and again as Mariska, Quinn, June, and their parents arrived. June, who'd been to my house many times before, ran inside the minute I opened the door and went off to play with the dogs. Mariska and Quinn, on the other hand, shyly followed their parents into our home. Rani and her parents were the last to arrive.

"Hi, Rani," I said when I held the door open.

"Hi," Rani said in a bored-sounding voice. She had also been to my home many times before, so she walked inside without me having to tell her to come in. Then she joined my sisters in the living room, where our guests were giving presents to the Wrights. Amber was the first to give them a present, actually, when she gave them the jasmine plant.

"Oh! It's lovely!" Mrs. Wright said.

"Thank you so much," Mr. Wright added. "What a thoughtful gift!"

"It might be good to plant this outside," Dad advised them. "That's what the man at the flower show said. The flowers bloom at night and the scent can be strong. He said it might be nice to plant it under a front window. That way the perfume can enter your home in the evenings."

"I love that idea!" Mrs. Wright said, raising the pot to admire the beauty of the plant.

"We have a gift too, don't we dear?" Mrs. Harrison nudged Rani closer to Jasmyn. "Why don't you give Jasmyn her little present?"

Rani's face was serious, without even the hint of a smile. "Here you go," she said, handing over a small package wrapped in golden paper.

I watched Jasmyn's face light up as she unwrapped it.

"I heard you've just signed up for dance classes," Mrs. Harrison said. "Now you have ruby slippers like the other girls."

Doesn't she mean 'red shoes'? I thought with a pang, and I glanced over at Rani to see if she was going to say anything to Jasmyn. But she didn't say a word.

I narrowed my eyes. *Has she even told her mother that she quit The Ruby Slippers?* It didn't look to me as if she had.

In fact, I hadn't told Jasmyn about the whole Ruby Slippers/ Red Shoes drama, either, so she was just thrilled with her present.

"Thank you!" she said, hugging the slippers to her heart.

Then the party got underway. The adults and the kids split into two groups, with the adults hanging out mostly in the living room and the kids in the sitting room.

But as the only high schooler in the group, Lena took turns hanging out with the adults and the kids. She also helped Aunt Sam in the kitchen and with serving snacks.

Ansley put the cinnamon rolls in to bake. She hadn't put them in the oven earlier because we all agreed that they were best served hot and fresh. Not to mention that the sweet cinnamony smell that filled the air when they were baking was better than any air freshener.

Since Mariska and Quinn loved baking, they joined her in

the kitchen. This left me, Amber, Jasmyn, Rani, and June in the sitting room.

I patted the seat next to me. "Why don't you sit with me, Rani?" I said and smiled at her. I wanted to show her that I still wanted to be friends even though she had quit my dance troupe. After all, staying friends with her was more important to me than having her stay in The Ruby Slippers. When she accepted my invitation and sat next to me, I felt hopeful even though she didn't return my smile. *Looks like she still wants to be friends,* I thought with a sigh of relief.

Next, I picked up the bowl of potato chips that was sitting on the coffee table and shook it at her. She took a couple of chips. Then I took a some and passed the bowl to Jasmyn. "When the others are done with the baking," I told her, "you can start your crocheting class." I turned to Rani. "We have the dining room all set up. It's going to be really cool. We're going to work on prayer shawls."

"I think we'll start with teaching you all how to make granny squares first," Jasmyn said. "It's best to start small so you can learn the basics."

"Yeah. Granny squares are pretty neat—" Amber began when Rani interrupted her.

"That sounds boring," she said and stood up. "I'm not doing that! Let's do something else." Rani looked out into the hall and at the staircase. "I know," she said to Amber. "Let's go to your room. There's neat stuff there." She didn't look at me, even though it was my room too.

Amber squirmed in her seat like she didn't know what to do or say.

I shook my head. "We can't," I said firmly.

But Rani went on, "They've got bunk beds, you know," she said to no one in particular. "Also, Ansley has a cool unicorn collection in her room upstairs."

I ground my teeth. "I just said we can't go upstairs. We're not going anywhere Jasmyn can't in her wheelchair."

But Rani ignored me. "Last one there is a rotten egg!" she yelled, and she ran out of the room.

Chapter 17

None of us spoke for a moment. Then I saw Jasmyn bite her lip. I hoped she wasn't going to cry.

Suddenly June sprang up from the couch like she was going to follow Rani, but I held out a hand to stop her. "No. I'll go get her," I said, and I stomped up the stairs to find Rani sitting on my bed. I wanted to tell her how mean I'd thought she'd been to Jasmyn when I heard her making sniffling sounds.

I sat down on the floor beside her and asked in a soft voice. "What's wrong?"

Rani wiped her face with her sleeve. "It turns out I *am* going to London! We're moving!"

"What?" My heart plunged to my stomach. "No! I thought your dad was still thinking about it."

"Well, he thought about it all right." Rani sniffed. Then she looked me over and sobbed, "Oh, don't act like you're sad about it. I know you won't even miss me!"

"What are you talking about? Of course I'll miss you!" I shook my head. "I don't want you to go. I never wanted you to go."

"I think you didn't at first," Rani said. "But then it didn't matter after you found *her*."

"Huh? Her who? You mean Jasmyn?"

Rani burst into tears.

I scrambled up off the floor and sat down beside her to put

my arm around her shoulders. "Do you think that I've replaced you with Jasmyn or something?"

Rani nodded. "Well, you have, haven't you? I mean, you're always with her. You have secrets together, visit each other's houses . . ."

"We're friends, yes, but it doesn't mean I don't have room in my heart for both of you. She can't take your place. You're both completely different people. Though you're both special to me."

"I used to be special. I used to be your dancing friend. But you're even dancing with Jasmyn, now, too."

"And June and Mariska and Quinn!" I reminded her. "Dance has brought us all together."

"And now England is going to take me away from all of you," Rani said in a tiny voice. "And you'll forget all about me."

"No! I could never do that!" I gave her arm a squeeze. "But you might forget us when you meet all those cool kids in London."

"No way!" Rani wiped her nose. "I'll always be your friend."

"Are you sure?" I had to ask. "Because the way you quit The Ruby Slippers and didn't want me dancing with you and Mariska and Quinn, I thought you didn't want to be my friend anymore."

"Oh," Rani looked sorrowful. "Did you really think that? I wanted you to beg me to stay in The Ruby Slippers. I wanted you to say you were going to forget all about Jasmyn and be my best friend again. But the truth is, Ashton, I never really wanted to quit The Ruby Slippers. Can I come back? Please?"

"Of course! You're the whole reason why I even started The Ruby Slippers in the first place! And you're still one my best friends," I said. "I hope you always will be."

Rani shook her head. "It will be too hard once I've moved. We won't be in the same school anymore, and we won't be able to go to each other' houses or to dance class together."

"I know," I said. "It will be hard. But we can still be friends. Like how Amber and I are friends with Giovanna."

"Who's Giovanna?" Rani asked with a confused laugh. "Oh, wait. Wasn't she your friend from Texas?"

"She still is my friend," I said. "That's my point. When I lived in Texas, we'd see each other in church and go over to each other's houses all the time. When I moved, I was sad to leave her and all my other friends behind. But God had plans for my family here. And part of that plan must have been for you and me to become friends. He must have plans for your family too. And friends in London He wants you to meet."

"Oh, Ashton. I wish you were moving to London too," Rani said with a sigh. She cupped her chin with her hands. "You always make me feel better."

"I can be in London. On your computer screen there, anyway," I said. "Amber and I video chat with Giovanna all the time. We can do that with you too."

"I'd like that," Rani said. "But you'll have to come and visit for *real* too!"

"And you can come and stay with us on vacation or something. We've got that guestroom downstairs . . . Oh! Speaking of guests and downstairs! I think we need to go back, don't you?"

"Yeah," Rani said, getting up and heading for my bathroom to wash her face. "I've been mean to Jasmyn. I've got to tell her I'm sorry."

By the time we were both downstairs we found all the girls

in the dining room. Lena was helping them set up for our crochet lesson.

Jasmyn watched suspiciously as Rani entered the room. Rani walked straight over to her and said in a sincere voice, "I don't think crocheting is boring. I really don't. I was just mad about something else. I'm sorry, Jasmyn. Please forgive me."

"It's okay," Jasmyn said, although she sounded a little unsure.

"I'd like to learn this before I move to London," Rani said in the same sad tone. But she couldn't go on because the table exploded with shock, surprise, and questions.

"But when are you going?" Mariska asked in a louder voice than the others. "Does this mean you won't be dancing in the talent show?"

Everyone listened with interest to the answer.

"No," Rani said. "Actually, Dad will be going over to London first to get things ready for us. Mom and I will stay a little longer so I can finish out the school year and she can take care of other things that have to do with the house."

Hearing her say that reminded me of when my family moved. There were so many details my parents had to take care that it made me glad that I was a kid and not a grown-up.

Rani sat in the chair closest to Jasmyn. "Please teach me how to make one of those granny thingies. If I learn how, maybe I can make a prayer shawl to take with me to London."

"I have an idea," Jasmyn said, looking around the table. "If you all learn to make granny squares, I can connect them together into one shawl. And you," she turned to Rani, "can take *that* with you to London."

"Hey, yeah! That way it's like you'll be wrapping yourself up in our prayers!" Amber said.

"And our hugs!" June said. "Whenever you want!"

"Really?" Rani looked very touched. "That would be so nice of you guys!"

Making a prayer shawl as a goodbye present for Rani made everyone even more excited to learn how to crochet. We all grabbed colored balls of yarn and crochet hooks. I looked for the coral pink ball of yarn I had chosen for myself when I was at Jasmyn's house, but I didn't see it anywhere. Then I saw Jasmyn dig into one of the side pockets of her powerchair. She pulled out the ball of yarn and handed it to me. "This one's yours," she said.

Then, when everybody was set with yarn and hooks, we all focused on Jasmyn expectantly.

"Okay, are you ready guys?" Jasmyn said. "Pay attention . . ."

Chapter 18

When the party was over, the last guests to go were Jasmyn and her parents.

"Don't go yet," Aunt Sam told them. "Let me pack some cinnamon rolls for you to take home."

"Oh, thank you!" Mrs. Wright clasped her hands together. "We'd love that!"

"How are there any left?" Mr. Wright asked in an amazed tone of voice. "They were awesome!"

"Oh, I hid these away for you," Aunt Sam explained. "Otherwise, you're right, there wouldn't be any left to give you."

Dad nodded. "It's true. Ansley's cinnamon rolls are always a hit."

While the adults chatted, my sisters and I sat in the living room with Jasmyn.

"I had a great time," Jasmyn told us. "Thank you for everything."

"We had a great time too!" Ansley said. "My granny square came out so cute!" She had used rainbow-colored yarn on her granny square. When Rani's prayer shawl was done, she would have no problem identifying which squares had been made by Ansley.

Dad came over with Mrs. Wright and sat by me. He had a curious expression on his face. "What's this I hear about you and Jasmyn dancing? Are you girls going to be in the talent show together?"

"No," I said. "I mean not unless something opens up. But we have been working on something. A dance to "God Is Good" by Mallory Winston."

Dad told the Wrights, "Mallory Winston is a family favorite. She's also a friend of ours."

"That's impressive," Mrs. Wright said. "We love her music too."

"The dance isn't ready yet," I told them all, "but when it is, maybe Jasmyn and I will perform it for all of you."

"You're doing a dance to "God Is Good?" Amber asked.

"Yes," I said.

"The song I'm supposed to sing?"

"Yes," I said again.

"Um . . . would the dance be ready in time for the talent show?" Amber asked next.

I nodded and said, "That's what we're aiming for. Just in case."

"Well, then, why don't you guys . . . that is, can't you . . ." Amber jumped to her feet. "Let's just share my slot at the talent show!"

"But Amber," I protested, "it should really be your solo!"

"But it will still be a solo," Lena pointed out. "You won't be singing with her, right? You'll be dancing. That means she'll be singing a solo."

"Exactly!" In her excitement, Amber hopped on one foot and then the other. "Don't you see? If you guys do your dance while I sing, I will still be singing alone on stage, but I won't *be* alone on stage! Oh! That would be perfect! Please say you'll do it!"

"Well . . . okay," I said. "If you really want us to. What do you say, Jasmyn?"

Jasmyn looked stunned. "Sure." She gulped. "But let's make sure to get in a lot of practice!"

Ansley grabbed a remote off the coffee table. Then, pretending it was a microphone, she started booming in her best announcer-type voice. "And for our next performance we will have that talented, up-and-coming singer, Amber Daniels, joined on stage by that dazzling, new, two-member dance troupe called The Ruby—"

I shook my head.

"Er, the Red—"

I shook my head again.

Ansley crossed her arms and tapped her foot. "Um, are you going to call yourselves something then, or just use your names?" she asked in her regular Ansley voice.

"Well, now that Jasmyn's got a pair of red slippers too, it'd be nice to have a name." I smiled down at Jasmyn's feet.

"Okay then. What's another name for red?" Jasmyn asked aloud.

"Crimson . . . scarlet . . . what about 'rose'?" Mrs. Wright suggested.

I perked up. "Rose? Isn't that more like pink?"

"Probably, but I was thinking more like rose red. You know, like ruby red."

I clapped my hands. "That's it! We can call ourselves The Rose Toes! Get it?"

Jasmyn laughed and nodded. "Yes, I get it! Rose Toes! It's cute and funny. Let's use it!"

"And now for our next performance . . ." Ansley began again.

And soon it actually *was* time for our talent show performance. Rani was super-nervous before going on stage. "Oh, why did I agree to dance in the middle?" she moaned.

"Don't worry," I told her. "You've got this. You're going to do fine. You're going to do great, even."

"I wish Dad wasn't still in London." Rani rubbed her arms like she was trying to scrape off the goosebumps that covered them. "Even though I know Mom is recording everything for him to watch later. It's not the same as knowing he's out there, rooting for me."

I began to fish in the pocket of my shorts. "Here," I said. "Will this help?" And from out of my pocket I took a little rock painted in sparkly pinks and purples. I HOPE YOU DANCE was written across its surface. "Does this look familiar?"

"Isn't this . . . ? Isn't this the rock I gave to you?"

"Yup. It's my favorite one. I've been keeping it in my room ever since coming up with the talent show idea. I used to look at it and pray that you'd get to perform in the talent show. And, well, here we are."

Rani looked down at the little rock in her palm. "You were going to dance with this in your pocket?"

"Well . . . yeah."

"Then you keep it," Rani said, handing it back to me. Her eyes shone. "You know . . . you're a good friend, Ashton."

"Thanks," I said, slipping the stone back inside my pocket. "So are you."

"All right then." Rani took a deep breath and grabbed one of my hands and one of June's. "I'm as ready as I'll ever be. Let's go!"

Lena had been right about performing on stage. There was something about being in front of a live audience that really inspired you to do your best. Maybe it was having all those eyes watching you in real time. Or knowing that there were no do-overs, like Amber had said. Whatever the reasons were, they helped The Ruby Slippers put on a good performance. And judging by the applause we received, the audience thought we did well too. I was really proud of us. When it was over and we were backstage again, Rani's face was flushed with excitement.

"That was fun!" she gushed. "I want to go back out there and do it all over again!"

And she got to, a little while later, when she joined The Red Shoes when they performed their dance. Her part wasn't as big in that one since she had joined them late. But Mariska and Quinn were very good dancers, and it turned out really well. I clapped for them all from the wings.

And it turned out that Amber and The Rose Toes were scheduled as the last act of the evening.

"Oh, no," Amber groaned when she saw the program. "Why? I just want to get this over with!"

She spent the entire time backstage hopping up and down, a jittery bundle of nerves. But when they finally announced us, she suddenly stopped bouncing and serenely led me and Jasmyn onto the darkened stage where we all took our places and waited for the music to begin.

Amber nodded to the stagehand in the wings, and soon

the familiar opening notes to "God Is Good" flowed from the speakers and filled the auditorium.

The spotlights came on, highlighting each of us, as Amber's voice rose clear and sure. She didn't sound nervous at all. She told me later that she closed her eyes a lot because it helped her to concentrate. I didn't notice, though, because I couldn't look at her. I had to focus on my dancing. (And it's not such a good idea to close your eyes when you're dancing on a stage.)

Dancing with Jasmyn was really special. I think we worked so well together because the song was something we both felt in our hearts. And we wanted the audience to feel it in their hearts too. And I guess they did, because when we were done, they gave us a standing ovation. The only standing ovation of the night.

While the audience was still clapping, I jogged over to Amber and gestured for her to hand me the microphone. Once she did, I cleared my throat. "I just wanted to say . . ." I began and waited for the applause to die down a little. "I just wanted to say," I repeated, "that Amber, Jasmyn, and I would like to dedicate that performance to our friend, Esperanza Harrison." There was a little cheer from a tiny section in the audience. *That must be where Rani's family is sitting,* I thought.

Amber took the microphone back from me and said, "We love you, Rani. And just want you to remember that through everything and all . . ."

"God is good!" Jasmyn, Amber, and I said together.

The audience applauded again as we lined up to take our bows. As I lowered my head, I imagined myself bowing before God in thanks. After all, just a few short weeks ago, this dance had been just a daydream. Now it had been performed in front of a real, live audience and the hit of the talent show. Now it was a dream that became a reality and a memory forever!

There's no doubt about it, I thought as I took another bow. *God is good.* I bowed again. *Good is good.* And again. *God is good.*

Amber's Song

Check out this excerpt from Book 3 in the Daniels Sisters Series

And there you go! Voila!" From her seat on the couch, my big sister, Lena, pronounced my hair done. "Take a look," she said. She passed her cell phone down to me.

I sat on the carpeted floor of my aunt's living room with my back to Lena. Taking the phone, I looked at the photo she'd snapped of the back of my head. Pretty braids covered my head in neat rows and flowed down my back.

I turned my head from side to side. "Wow!" I grinned. "Nice job, Lena."

Our Aunt Trini, who was sitting next to Lena on the couch, smiled proudly at both of us. "You're good with your hands, Lena. Maybe it's from all that guitar playing. It looks like you'll be an expert at braiding hair in no time."

Lena shook her head. "I only did okay because you were right next to me. Without you showing me what to do—or fixing my mistakes—her hair would never have come out this nice."

"Well, I am a professional hairstylist," Aunt Trini reminded her. "I have had years of experience. But that's why you should believe me when I say you did a good job."

"Okay," Lena said with a small smile.

Springing to my feet, I handed the phone back to Lena just as Aunt Trini gave me a hand mirror to look into. I checked my braids out again and flipped some with my free hand. "Even though I'm not a professional," I said, "I think they look great too. Thanks, Lena! I really love them!"

"And while they're very pretty," Aunt Trini said, taking the mirror back from me, "they will also be practical for camp. The braids will keep your hair out of your face when you're doing sports. But don't forget what I told you about washing your hair and protecting it with conditioner before going into the pool."

"I won't," I promised.

Aunt Trini sifted through my braids playfully. "And you can always tie them in a long—not to mention fabulous—ponytail when you want to."

"A 'fabulous ponytail!'" I laughed and jokingly did a small runway walk in front of the couch. I ended it with a toss of my head that flipped my braids behind my back. "Fabulous!"

I heard laughter from my two sisters who were sitting on the other couch. I looked over at them. But something about the way they giggled made me know they weren't laughing at my goofing around. They were laughing about something else.

Then I saw the reason! Middle-sister Ansley and my twin sister, Ashton, were sitting side-by-side on the couch just like Lena and Aunt Trini were. Only they were weaving tiny, funny-looking braids into our dad's short, curly hair. They were also clipping pink, sparkly barrettes on the end of each braid. Dad didn't know, because even though he was sitting on the floor, like I had been, his eyes were closed and he was taking slow, deep breaths. He had fallen asleep! I clapped both hands over my mouth and giggled.

Dad, my sisters, and I were all staying at Aunt Trinity's house in Texas for a few weeks that summer. She had spent a lot of our visit showing us sisters how to style each other's hair in different ways. We needed to learn for ourselves because our mom used to know lots of ways to style our hair and sadly she had died last year. We really missed not having her around to love us and teach us about God. But we also missed the smaller things she used to do for us—like our hair. Dad's sister, our aunt Samantha, lived with us now. And she did our hair most of the time when we were home in Tennessee. But Aunt Trini had taught Mom how to do hair years ago so she decided that she was going to teach us girls too. At least as much as she could during our visit. The braids on my father's head, though, made it look like some of us needed more practice!

Trying to be as quiet as possible, I waved in Lena's face, held a finger up to my lips, and pointed over at Dad. Lena and Aunt Trini both caught sight of his new hairdo just as the doorbell rang.

Dad's eyes flew open. He scrambled to his feet. "I'll get it," he mumbled.

We sisters squealed with laughter.

Aunt Trini stood up. "Um, wait, why don't I . . . ?"

But in a few long strides, Dad had already made it to the front door. "Hello, Gio!" we heard him say.

"Hi there. . . Mr. . . . Daniels." A familiar voice replied. The surprised quiver in her voice made it sound like she was trying not to laugh.

Ashton and I gasped. "Giovanna!" we said together and ran for the door.

Giovanna Rossi was an old friend of ours from when we used

to live in Texas. Since we moved away right after our mother died, we hadn't seen her in person for a year. She had come to stay at our aunt's house that night so that we could all get an early start to camp the next day. Dad was going to drive us.

When Ashton and I reached the front door, we saw Gio grinning widely as she stared up at our father's hairdo.

"Oh!" Dad brought a hand up to the top of his head and he began touching the barrettes. He burst out laughing. "As you can see, I just came from the salon."

"It's really you," Mrs. Rossi said in an amused voice.

"I like to stay on trend," Dad joked. "Come in, come in." He opened the door wider.

"Oh, is it okay if I don't? I have Mr. Rossi waiting in the car." Mrs. Rossi gestured behind her.

"No worries." Dad took Giovanna's trunk from her mother's hand. "Come on in, Gio."

After giving her mother a quick kiss and hug goodbye, Gio ran toward me and Ashton. She squealed. I squealed. Ashton squealed. Then we all took each other's hands, jumped up and down, and squealed some more.

When we stopped jumping and squealing, Gio panted. "I've missed you guys so much!"

"We've missed you too," I said, still holding her hands and swinging them back and forth. "Come on! We'll show you where you'll be sleeping."

We brought Gio to a little study on the ground floor that had a daybed with a pullout bed underneath it. "You can sleep on the top or the bottom or on the inflatable mattress." Ashton pointed to the cardboard box that was leaning against the wall near the doorway. "It's just not inflated yet."

"It doesn't matter to me," Gio said, flopping herself down on the floor. "I can sleep anywhere. Sleeping is like my hobby." She laughed.

It was true. Last year at camp, Gio was always the first to fall asleep, the last to wake up. Ashton usually fell asleep pretty easily too. I know because I was usually the last one to fall asleep. I didn't like the dark. And I couldn't sleep unless I kept a night-light on.

My night-light! Did I remember to pack it? I wondered. I'd better check. I had meant to bring my night-light from home. It was shaped like a little cat and it gave off a warm, cheerful glow when it was plugged in. I hadn't checked to make sure I had packed it before because I hadn't needed it the past few days. Once Ashton and I were in bed, Aunt Trini always left our bedroom door open a crack with a dim light on in the hallway for us.

I dragged out my trunk from under a nearby desk and began to look through its compartments. Hmm. Not in the front pocket . . . not in the side pocket . . . not in the other side pocket. Gosh, I hope I didn't leave it back home! I felt my heart begin to thump fast. I unzipped the small pouch that held my toothbrush and toothpaste with shaking hands and began to search through it. No night-light. Maybe it's somewhere under all my clothes. I sighed deeply. The only way to make sure was to take out everything Aunt Sam had neatly packed and what I had secretly packed. I tried to hide what I was doing from Ashton, who was busy chatting with Gio, but it was impossible. I took out a stack of T-shirts, some pairs of shorts, some sneakers.

Ashton stopped talking to Gio and frowned. "What are you do—?" Then she let out a tiny gasp as she caught sight of something soft and white in my suitcase. "You packed your kitty coat? In the middle of summer?"

My "kitty coat" was a fluffy, white, fake-fur jacket that had been the last present my mother had given me. When it was new, I wore it practically every day and Mom started calling me her "fluffy little kitty" whenever she saw me. She would even pet me by stroking my "fur" as I snuggled up against her. Soon "fluffy little kitty" got shortened to just "kitty." And it became Mom's special nickname for me. Nowadays Kitty was the nickname my whole family called me at home.

"Yes . . . " I said. But seeing the look of disbelief on Ashton's face made my face burn. I turned away from her and suddenly noticed my cat night-light tucked in the side of the suitcase, protected by some rolled-up socks. Feeling a wave of relief pass over me, I snatched it up and gave it a little hug. Then I began covering up my coat with the T-shirts and shorts I had just taken out of the suitcase.

"When do you think you're going to get the chance to wear it at camp?" Ashton went on. "Plus, it's going to get so dirty if you do!" She turned to Gio. "Can you believe that? She packed a coat for a Texas summer camp!" Then she turned back to me only to shake her head. "Did you already forget how ridiculously hot it gets here in the summertime?"

I felt my heart clutch a little. I knew everything she had said was right, but I didn't care. "Our cabins are air-conditioned," I said, still not looking at her. "You know how cool they can get. I can wear the coat like . . . a kind of robe."

From the corner of my eye, I could see Ashton shake her head again. "You should have just brought a robe then."

Even though we were twins, Ashton and I were not the

identical kind. We didn't look alike and our personalities were quite different.

For instance, Ashton was more serious than me. She could also be very practical, which is why she didn't understand why I would want to bring my fluffy coat to camp. She probably even thought it was silly of me. (I could be silly sometimes! It made life more fun!) But I wasn't bringing the coat with me to be silly. It was just that sometimes wearing it made me feel like I was getting hugs from my mom. Plus, Mom had given me the coat more than a year ago. I had grown since then. And although I wasn't *much* bigger than I was the year before, I was taller than Ashton now—and even Ansley—so I had the feeling that it wouldn't be much longer before I grew out of my coat. I wanted to wear it every chance I could. Even if I had to sleep in it!

Suddenly Gio laughed. "I really did miss you guys!" she said looking back and forth from me to Ashton.

"We missed you too!" Ashton and I said together. We got on either side of Gio and hugged her.

"Twin cuddles!" Gio said. She wrapped an arm around each of us and gave us a squeeze.

When we broke apart, Gio jumped up and pointed to the small, curvy case that leaned against the wall near the door. "What is that? A tiny guitar or something?"

"It's a ukulele," I said. I snatched it up and brought it over to show her. After I unzipped the case, I showed it to her and plucked a few strings. "See?"

"So basically, yeah, a tiny guitar," Gio said, with a grin. She looked me over with wide and shining eyes. "I didn't know you could play!"

"Yeah, well, Lena's been teaching me."

"Maybe you'll get the chance to be a leader of song or something," Gio said, running a figure lightly over the ukulele strings. The theme at camp this year was "All Creation Sings Praise," which, according to the brochure, meant that there would be singing classes as well as outdoor sports and nature activities. "You know," Gio continued as I put the uke back in the case, "since you got to sing that solo at the talent show."

I kind of wanted to just curl up in a blanket and hide when she said that. I mean, actually at first it felt like my heart grew wings and zoomed up my chest at her words. Part of me loved-loved-loved the idea of singing on stage. And wanted to do it again as soon as possible. But another part of me froze up inside at the very idea of having to perform in front of a lot of people. On the day of the school talent show that she mentioned, I had been so nervous that I thought I was going to throw up before I sang! (I didn't.) What ended up helping me a lot was that Ashton was on stage with me that day. She didn't sing—she danced. But at least I hadn't been all alone up there. I shrugged at Gio's suggestion. "Maybe." I put the ukulele case on top of the desk. "I'm not bringing it with me. It's Lena's," I explained.

"Girls!" Aunt Trini called from the kitchen down the hall. "Anyone for some freshly popped popcorn?"

Gio, Ashton, and I all exchanged glances. *Anyone? Make that all of us!* "Coming!" we all yelled together, and we ran out of the room.

www.ingramcontent.com/pod-product-compliance
Ingram Content Group UK Ltd.
Pitfield, Milton Keynes, MK11 3LW, UK
UKHW022332180625
459827UK00001B/135

9 780310 769613